An interesting footnote to
that young Irelander, Tho:
America in 1848 via Culd
Gee—disguised as a clerg
passage was secured for h
1858 he had established the 'New Era' newspaper in which
he advocated the creation of a Canadian nation. On July
1st 1867, he was a member of the Canadian legislature
which admitted New Brunswick as one of the four original
provinces of the Dominion of Canada.

As I followed the turbulent life and times of Cassie O'
Connor from County Donegal to New Brunswick, I was
reminded of T. S. Elliot's lines;

> "Beneath the bleeding hands we feel
> The sharp compassion of the healer's art
> Resolving the enigma of the fever chart."

Cassie's life parallels an equally convulsive period in
famine Ireland but Hazel Mc Intyre doesn't resort to easy
cliché or cosy familiarity. Her's is 'the healer's art'; the
British and Irish are not conveniently brutal and
downtrodden in equal measure; 'the fever chart' of
Ireland's history is much too enigmatic to be used as a
expedient backdrop for a work of fiction. There is
suffering in 'Lament In The Wind' but the innate
compassion of the author ensures that we are left with hope
and affirmation. This is a love story and to quote Anthony
Trollope; 'Those who have courage to love should have
courage to suffer.'

Frank Galligan writer and broadcaster BBC Radio.

Iris.

Lament in the Wind

Hazel Mc Intyre

Hazel Mc Intyre

Moran Publications

First published in Ireland by
Moran Publications
1998

ISBN   0-9524426-1-2

Typeset: Stuart Clarke
Cover Illustration: James McLaughlin

Printed and bound in Ireland by:
Browne Printing, Letterkenny, Co Donegal.

I would like to thank all my family and friends for their
Support and encouragement, particularly my husband
Charles, Jan Mc Guinness, Sean Beattie,
Marie Mc Keeney, Michelle Mc Cole,
and all my good friends in
Inishowen and Derry.

To The memory of all those who died and were
forced to emigrate during the Great Hunger;
I would like to dedicate

Lament in the Wind

Hazel Mc Intyre was born on a farm in the Innishowen peninsula of Co. Donegal in Ireland. After leaving school she moved to London where she became a nurse, before marrying husband Charles. They later moved back to Ireland, where they now live with their three children.

Her first book 'Iron Wheels On Rocky Lanes' which vividly recalled her Donegal childhood was first published in 1994 to an outstanding ovation from the critics. Her first work of fiction 'For Love Of Mary Kate' was published in 1996 and told the powerful and compelling tale of three generations of women in 1920's rural Ireland. It was hailed by newspaper critics as 'the first of many fine novels from this emerging Donegal writer.'

In addition to her role as writer, housewife and Mother Hazel Mc Intyre runs creative writing classes, gives talks to woman's groups, support groups also radio and television interviews both in Ireland, the USA and Canada.

Contents

Chapter 1

Mary's Journey

The flight from Shannon to New York was right on time. Mary Simpson waited impatiently in the queue clutching the bag containing the diaries closely. She was a tall unconsciously beautiful, young woman with black hair and deep set green eyes. On the surface of things she had everything she wanted, a successful career as the editor of a famous glossy magazine, and a beautiful apartment in a fashionable area of New York. She was artistic in ways that always amazed her friends, and yet she felt that something was missing in her life. The endless search for trivial news and glamorous photographs of the rich and famous had become more and more unfulfilling and meaningless to her. The same questions, the same answers, and the constant search to fool the readers into thinking that they were reading something new and unique about their idols.

Then she thought of Andy who would be waiting

for her at Kennedy Airport; she could picture his lanky image vividly in her head; his crisp blonde hair, his big blue-grey eyes, his powerful shoulders and a smile that had the power to turn her legs to jelly. Yet, she was unwilling to make a firm commitment about their future together. But she also knew that she cared deeply about him.

As the aircraft lifted higher, she gazed at the patchwork quilt pattern of greens, and the winding Shannon far below, her thoughts went back to her grandmother and the treasures she had entrusted to her.

At the age of seventy, she had returned to Donegal, in the North West of Ireland to spend her remaining years, and now ten years on, and crippled with arthritis she was confined to a nursing home. This had been Mary's fourth visit in the past year, and each time she noticed her grandmother becoming more feeble and yet she stubbornly resisted any mention of returning to New York. The closeness to her grandmother had increased after the untimely death of her mother from cancer three years earlier, and on top of this blow had come her father's announcement that he was getting married again. She simply could never forgive him for this act of betrayal to her mother's memory and had refused to go to the wedding or, to meet her stepmother. She had met her father on a couple of occasions since then at a neutral venue, and on the condition he came alone. These meetings had been cold affairs because she stubbornly rejected any mention of his new wife.

"I want you to make peace with your father, Mary. It's what your mother would want and what I want," her grandmother had said to her a few hours earlier.

"I haven't a lot of time left, and I want you to do this, if only for me," she had urged.

"I'll try Grandma," she had promised. But she knew, that she still felt too hurt and angry to forgive him. It was then that, she finally handed over her grandmother's diaries that she had talked to her about all her life.

"You are the one I am entrusting these to. I know that they will be in safe keeping," she had said, as her old eyes misted over. "There is the history from a century and a half ago inside these pages. It tells her own story and the story of all those around her."

"I know what a treasure you have entrusted to me Grandma. And I will use it well."

"I wouldn't have given them to you if I didn't believe that. And I am the only one left that remembers her. You have the same green eyes you know. Although, I only remember her as an old woman, yet I can still see those beautiful green eyes. And, remember it's not a sad story. It's a story of love and courage that you must tell, so that future generations will know."

"I promise."

Mary sat and held her hand until she fell asleep.

Now over the Atlantic Ocean she carefully opened the diaries that Cassie O' Connor began writing almost one hundred and fifty years earlier.

Only when the aeroplane wheels hit the tarmac did she lift her head; so captivated had she been in the lives, of the people who had lived through another time, so very far removed from her own, and yet she felt that she knew each one intimately.

In the terminal building she collected her luggage as though in a daze. In her mind she was in that other world living with her great-great grandmother and those who impacted so deeply on her life and times. Then she saw Andy waiting for her with that lopsided smile of welcome. "Great to see you," he boomed, bending down to kiss her. As if emerging from a coma, she regarded him with vague, unseeing eyes and made a visible effort to drag herself back to the present.

"How was your grandmother?"

"Pretty feeble," she answered vacantly, her mind still on another time and place.

As they made their way towards the car park, he asked,

"Are you doing the Cannes Film Festival this time?" She shook her head, and made no reply. Places like the Cannes Film Festival and all that it entailed somehow seemed so trivial now.

Leaving the airport behind, he drove out onto the freeway. Glancing at her again, he noticed that far away expression, and asked, "what's up honey? You seem so distant."

"I have something to tell you Andy," she said suddenly, looking across at him. "You are not going to like it much. But, I've made up my mind." Without replying he pulled the car into the nearest service station and switched off the engine. With a deepening frown on his face he asked, "what is it Mary? Out with it."

Still nursing the diaries, she opened the black bag and took one out, "it's these," she said. She gazed into space for a minute, and then she told him of her grandmother and the diaries of Cassie O'Connor.

"I'm going back to Ireland for a year or more to write. This is a story that has been entrusted to me. It must be told. I want it to be a small tribute to Cassie O'Connor, and to the courage of the human spirit. My grandmother hasn't a great deal of time left. And I want her to read the finished book before she dies. If I can do a good enough job on it to meet with her approval... that's all I want to achieve," she ended lamely, as though she didn't expect him to understand.

They stared at each other in silence for a while. Then he said quietly, "you'll do a good job of it. Could I come to visit you occasionally? And maybe help you from time to time, with research and that."

Her lips parted in a smile, and she threw her arms around his neck.

"How soon can we start on your book?"

"Right away. I must start now while it's all in my

head." Then, looking deeply into his eyes, she said quietly, "and when the book's finished, then we'll talk about us. And I want you to be there for me when my grandmother reads the finished work."

"I'll be there for you," he said, kissing her gently on the lips.

Chapter 2

Donegal 1850

Apart from the lament of the wind, there was silence in the gloomy kitchen. Cassie O'Connor, looked across at the silent figure of her mother Ellen, huddled over the dying embers of the fire.

"Will I get more sticks?" she asked. Her mother nodded. Cassie didn't really expect her to answer; in fact she hadn't spoken since her father drowned three weeks earlier.

She emerged from the low doorway, and hastily glanced at the little huddled houses, showing stark against the bright blue sky. She was small and skinny for her ten years, with a shock of unkempt black curling hair, and a small pinched face making her round green eyes look too big, giving her a haunted appearance.

She climbed up the slope to the whin hill, and began breaking off the dead thorny branches. When she had broken off an armful, she straightened her back, and looked out towards the ocean. The sun was dropping on the far horizon; its last beams making a blood-red pathway across the turbulent Atlantic waters. The pangs of hunger made her stagger, as she bent down to pick up the sticks. The stormy sea meant that the fishing boats wouldn't be out, and that meant no fish. She went to the port on calm evenings in the hope that one of the fishermen would take pity on her, and give her a couple of herring, or whatever was spare. And they mostly did. But unless Johnny Molly brought them some milk, she would have to go to bed with the pains of hunger again. Cassie recalled that she had been hungry since her father died. When the potatoes failed, he had to give up his job as a teacher, and become a fisherman. The fish he caught kept them fed; until three weeks ago. The memory of him came to her now clearly; strong safe arms reaching towards her in a thankful grasp. She saw his laughing green eyes, so much like her own, and the strong gentle reassurance that made her ache with love for him. But the memory always slid away when she tried to catch it.

She stumbled back down the hill, with her burden of sticks, held by skinny, scratched, and blood stained arms. As she rounded the gable of the house, she saw the two horses. A man in a red coated uniform stood silently between them holding the reins. Dropping the sticks at her feet, she stood watching, her face, as pale as death, mirroring the terror in her soul. She could hear a man's loud voice coming from within. She ran inside, distraught. "Please, don't put us out ...please," she added, in a near whisper. He turned around to face her, and heaved a deep sigh.

"I have a job to do. If you pay the back rent you can stay."

"We have no money. My father's dead, and we're famished," her small voice trailed away. Going over closer to where Ellen sat, he looked down at her for a while in silence.

"If you're hungry now, then there's no chance of you surviving the winter. Go to the workhouse. That's all's for you."

Ellen stared at the dead fire without comment, her pale thin face, and tragic eyes making her seem barely alive. It was a sight to appeal to the better instincts of any man, but this was not permitted to sway John Brown, in pursuit of what he called his duty. Then swinging around to Cassie again, he asked, "why won't she speak, for God's sake. I haven't all day to stand around here."

"She hasn't spoken since my Daddy was drowned."

"Look, either you go to the workhouse, or you pay the rent."

"No we won't. We won't," cried Cassie in a half sob.

From the door he turned again to face her, before adding, "you have one week from now."

When he had gone, Cassie slumped down to the floor, and listened to the sound of the horse's hooves fade into the distance. She sat there rocking to and fro, with strange small sounds, coming from her throat.

She was still sitting in the same position, when Johnny Molly came in ten minutes later. Bending down, he took her small hand in his and gently pulled her to her feet.

"What happened? Are they going to evict you?" she nodded. "He gave us a week to get the rent. He says we will have to go to the workhouse. Said we would be fed there."

"Damn him to hell. Damned bastards." Nodding towards her mother, he asked, "has she spoken yet?"

"Not a word."

"Poor wee Cassie, poor wee Cassie," he repeated, rubbing her head. "I brought some milk, and a bit of bread. We'll get the fire lit and see if we can't get some life back into her, eh!"

After she had eaten her own bread and drank her milk, she looked across to where her mother sat. She hadn't touched her bread or the milk. She just stared at the whin sticks as they crackled and flamed, lighting up her pale drawn face. Going over to where she sat, Johnny stood between her and the fire.

"Listen to me," he said, grabbing her shoulders. "You are going to eat this bread and drink the milk. By God you are, even if I have to stay here all night. It's your duty to live, and look after your waine. Do you hear me?" he half shouted. Suddenly, she lifted her eyes to meet his. He handed her the milk, and she lifted it slowly to her mouth and drank. "That's more like it. Now eat this bread. I'm not leaving 'till you do." She took the piece of bread from his outstretched hand, and began to eat it slowly. When she had finished eating he said, "I want to help you more than anything else I ever wanted to do before. But I don't know how. I have no money to pay your rent for you, and I have barely enough food to feed my own six mouths."

Before the pangs of hunger began again, Cassie got into bed, closed her eyes, and let blessed sleep blot out her fears.

When she awoke, her mother was standing in front of the open door, staring straight ahead. A blast of cold wind made her grab the door to steady her fragile frame. The light from the door lit up her father's straw bag of books. For a moment, she almost forgot that he was dead. Suddenly turning around, her mother spoke. The sound of her voice made Cassie jump; she had almost forgotten what her voice sounded like, and the surprise of it caused her not to hear what she actually said.

"What did you say?" she asked her.

"I said I want you to get up and wash yourself. We will go to the workhouse while we have the strength to make it."

Jumping out of bed, Cassie ran to her and threw her arms around her waist.

"You've come back, you've come back."

"Save your strength Cassie. We have a seven mile walk ahead of us."

Carrying the small bag of books in one hand and Cassie their few other possessions they set off up the laneway. At the top of the hill, Ellen stood looking back at the small cluster of cabins huddled under the hillside. Turning her head to the right, she gazed at the rugged windswept shore, far below the white foamy waves lashed against the rocks in a fury. Cassie watched while her mother's lips moved. But there was no sound.

Three miles along the way, they sat down sandwiching themselves between the fuchsia hedge for shelter against the biting wind. Feeling too weak to go on, they became aware of someone standing over them.

"Where you heading for?" a male voice asked. Looking up they saw a thin bearded man eyeing them curiously.

"The workhouse.... If we make it," Ellen answered meeting his steady gaze. "You'll need a bite to eat, or you won't make it. If you follow me home I'll get something in your stomachs."

Getting up slowly, the cold biting wind making them hunch deeper into their ragged coats, they stumbled along behind him. At the foot of a rocky hill he turned right along a grass track, that led to his home; a cave, almost hidden under the rocks.

Inside it was warm with a glowing turf fire.

"Sit down, and get warmed up. When you get some of this fish soup inside you, you'll feel revived." They watched him put pieces of fish and green herbs into the pot, then, hang it over the glowing coals. "I have lived here for six years now. It's hardly a palace. But at least I have no rent to pay; no fear of the dreaded bailiff." Turning his head around to face them he asked, "were you evicted?" Ellen nodded. Turning back to stir the pot, he muttered inaudibly in Irish before turning to face them again. "It's a bad time that has come on our proud and noble race. But, our time will come again. The workhouse isn't a good place to be heading for. But it will keep you living 'till the spring." Then he carefully poured the fish broth into three bowls, and handing one to each of them, he said, "drink every drop. It will put new life into you." He sat silently staring into space while they drank the broth. Ellen remembered the last time she had been to this place, and Michael telling her about the man who lived in the cave who, had been evicted. He had also told her that his wife and child died in childbirth. As they sat in the dark cave, Ellen sensed his pain. She could not think of any words of comfort, so they sat in a rather uncertain silence.

They rested for an hour before going on their way. Along the way, they saw endless deserted homesteads, here and there ragged hungry children scavenged berries from the bushes by the roadside. The devastation of the past five years, since the potato blight first struck was all around them, making their spirits sink even lower.

Chapter 3

At the Workhouse Door

Marcia Briggs, daughter of the Reverend Henry Briggs, sat in the pony trap, waiting patiently for her father, to reappear from the stark grey building that was the workhouse. She had begged him to let her accompany him inside.

"No, Marcia. The fever is rampant; it's highly contagious. Six people have perished in the last two days," he said.

"But I want to be of some help. Please," she added.

"No. If I lost you I couldn't go on." His face looked grey and curiously older, but his eyes were kind. "I won't be long," he said, getting out of the trap, and heading towards the door. As she watched his back disappear inside the door, a feeling of tenderness and gratitude towards him swept over her. Had he not persuaded her, to help him with his work, she would have gone half crazy with grief by now, she was sure. Alone she waited, and her thoughts went back to Johnny.

Within the space of a few months she had fallen in love with him, and now she didn't even know if he was alive or dead. It seemed a lifetime since she had seen him on the shore; his lopsided grin, and mop of black hair brought his presence near in her mind. She could picture him clearest in the boat shed where he worked, making and repairing the fishing boats; she could again smell the wood shavings, and the pain of longing almost took her breath away.

It all ended so suddenly when her mother caught them in an intimate embrace. As a punishment, her mother had locked her in her room. She had found that he had gone three days later, when she escaped from her room through the window, and scrambled down through the branches of the oak tree, by the side of the house. She had run as fast as her legs could carry her, to Johnny's cottage close to the shore. Standing close to the door, she stopped for breath. All seemed strangely quiet, and as she stood there in the twilight a feeling of foreboding came over her. She knocked on the door and went in. When her eyes had adjusted to the gloom, she saw his elderly parents sitting silently at either side of the fire. Clearing her throat loudly, she asked, "where is Johnny?" Two sets of hostile eyes turned to stare at her. A period of silence followed, before his mother said, "Johnny has gone.... I know not where. Might even be dead," she added, with a deep sadness in her dull voice.

"What do you mean.... gone? Why would he go? Why might he be dead?" she screeched, close to hysteria.

"Don't tell me you didn't know. The redcoats made a lift of him in the dead of night."

Turning to face her, his father spoke for the first time, "ask that damned family of yours. They're the ones that had him lifted. I wish he'd never set eyes on you. Oh, God.... How I wish he'd never set eyes on you." She ran from the house in anguish, her tears almost blinding her eyes. Only when she reached the rectory did she stop for breath. Padding through the house with noiseless feet, she opened the drawing room door and saw her parents sitting silently close to the fire. Suddenly the anger and pain she was feeling burst like a bubble.

"Where is Johnny? Where did they take him?" she screamed, as her father's startled gaze met hers. Getting up from his chair, he crossed the space between them in a few strides.

"Marcia, Marcia... what is it? What's wrong?" Pounding against his chest with clenched fists, she screeched, "you know damned well what you did. It was you who sent the redcoats. He might even be dead. I love him.... do you hear me? I love him."

Grabbing her shoulders, and shaking them gently, he said in a loud stern voice, "I don't know what you're talking about. I know nothing about redcoats or Johnny... who ever he is. Do you here me?"

As his honest, bewildered grey eyes met hers, it

suddenly dawned on her that he was telling the truth.

They simultaneously, looked across to where Julia Briggs sat. A look of guilt came into her cold blue eyes, as she averted them from their gaze, and began picking threads from her embroidery with thin, nervous fingers, keeping her eyes lowered. Going over to where she sat, Marcia said in an anguished whisper, "it was you.... my God it was you. Where is he? Please.... please tell me," she pleaded, falling down on her knees in front of her.

"Marcia, I had no option but to have him removed. He is no match for you.... He would wreck your life. Don't you see that, darling?"

"Where is he? Where did... they take him?" Her voice trailed away in an anguished sob. "I don't know where he is. John Brown saw to it. I honestly don't know. But, you will thank me in the long run."

Henry Briggs looked down at his wife, his pale, cold eyes directed just above her head, and in a voice full of contempt, he said, "you had no right to do such a thing Julia. You had no right." He repeated.

"I had every right. Johnny McFarland was no match for our daughter. You would have done nothing as always, even if I had told you," she shouted back, defiantly.

Looking down at Marcia, he asked, "is it Johnny McFarland, the boat builder?" Not lifting her head, from where she sat slumped on the floor, she nodded silently.

"God help us. I know the McFarlands. He's their

only son." Then looking back at his wife, he said, "what were you thinking about? And using that damned Brown, when you know how I despise the man, is beyond belief."

"I did what I had to," Julia repeated, getting up from her chair. As their eyes met, the hostility between them soured the air. With a final defiant stare, she walked from the room. When she had gone Henry got down on the floor beside Marcia. As he looked at her small, tragic, almost childlike face, he felt a deep pity stir in him.

"I will confront Brown tomorrow, and see what I can get out of him. Then I'll go to his parents," he added with a deep sigh.

They talked deep into the night. As dawn broke, Marcia felt at last, that she could sleep. Holding out his arms, Marcia walked into them, and felt the comfort of his compassion ease the sadness in her heart. As she felt the rough surface of his old tweed jacket against her hot cheek, she experienced a deep love for her father, such, as she had never known before.

Now, sitting alone in the trap, she felt overcome with the frustration of helplessness, both for her own loss, and the tragedy that was all around her. This evening she would make her way to the cottage at the shore, as she had done for months, hoping each time that they would have news of Johnny's whereabouts. But, each time she was to be disappointed. His parents would shake their heads, almost as soon as she reached the door.

All her father could force from John Brown, was that he was put on a ship for North America. Marcia, filled her days helping her father with his work; and all the while her heart ached. She wanted to be someone other than the Marcia Briggs, who had never been treated as an adult in her own right. For as far back as memory would take her, she had been told what to do and when to do it. Inside she wanted to break free, to do something outrageous even shocking. The anger at her mother's actions burned deep inside her and would not be quelled.

As she sat still, lost in meditation and loneliness, gazing at the cold starkness of the workhouse, her attention was suddenly caught by two figures approaching the gates. Ragged and weak, they stumbled towards the door.

Jumping out of the trap, she ran towards them, "no, no, don't go in. There's an outbreak of fever," she called. Standing beside them, she suddenly wondered what she would do next.

Where else could they go? Then, in a sudden flash she thought that this was the chance to prove herself, the chance she had been waiting for. She could put them in the room above the kitchen she decided in a sudden instant. That her motives were selfish didn't in that moment cause her any great concern; she was fired inside by the burning need to do something unpredictable, something that would send her mother into a frenzy.

"Come over to the trap. I'll look after you back at the rectory," she said guiding them towards the trap. As she helped them into the trap, her father reappeared.

"What's this Marcia? What are you doing?" he asked from behind her.

"They were about to go in there. They wouldn't survive a week. The fever would take them in no time in their weak condition. I'll look after them at home until they're stronger."

"But your mother. You know how she'll react."

"I don't care how she'll react. I must try to save their lives." They stood in silence looking at each other solemnly, and then he said, "all right Marcia, I'm on your side. Let's get going before darkness falls."

Marcia smiled inwardly in triumph. She felt in control of something for once in her life, and that her actions would get at least a little revenge on her mother made it all the sweeter. She was not to know then how much her life would change, because of her sudden action.

The pony took off at a smart trot between the hedges, topping an earth wall at each side of the road, then at the steep ascent before the shore the pony dropped into a walk. Ellen and Cassie sat huddled together, as if in a trance; their eyes held a haunted and fearful look that mirrored the fear of the unknown that lay ahead.

The old familiar scent of honeysuckle came to Ellen from the hedgerow, and enveloped her like a magic cloak, transporting her back through the years to a time when life was sweet. Michael's face came before her now, and his loss, and that of her two infant sons, made her heart weep with longing. Ellen's memories were locked deep within her body and were for her an ever present ache.

Cassie stole a fearful glance at the strange young woman seated opposite her. As their eyes met, she smiled at her with kindness in her face. Somehow, in that moment Cassie felt at ease, and her dread began to evaporate a little.

Henry Briggs, lost in thought, looked at the woman and child in their misery and distress with compassion in his heart for their plight. Their plight was a poignant reminder of the starkness of the tragedy, that surrounded them, and of his calling, and faith that had been sorely tested. And yet, he had never regretted his calling to the ministry, in spite of the helplessness that was part of his everyday lot. He hated the system, that brought this misery on the people that he had grown to love; yet he was painfully aware of the fact, that he was also part of that very system.

As they neared the overgrown driveway, thoughts of his wife Julia caused him to shudder, and sigh deeply. He could well imagine her hostile reaction to the newcomers. He wondered again why he had ever married her. He knew that she was selfish to the core, with no compassion in her soul. Yet he had married her, and he must remain the dutiful spouse, true to his marriage vows. Relations between them had worsened since the episode with Johnny. He hated having to depend on his in-laws in England, at least in part, for survival. Julia reminded him of this fact almost on a daily basis, and it hurt. And yet, he had his two children, and for that blessing alone he owed her gratitude.

It was now almost dark, and the bold outline of the mountain range looked hauntingly repellent cast in religious black. When the pony stopped at the door, he jumped down and helped them alight from the trap. Before opening the front door, he turned to Ellen and said,

"please try to ignore my wife. She won't... exactly welcome you with open arms. But both Marcia and myself will do all we can to make you feel at home." Taking her hand in his, he squeezed it gently, and opened the door. Inside, the hall was brightly lit by two oil lamps, which contrasted sharply with the near darkness outside. Cassie, blinking in the sudden brightness, saw a door open, and a beautifully dressed woman stood in front of them.

"What is the meaning of this Henry? Get them out of here," she shrieked. Taking a hankie out of her pocket, she put it over her mouth and nose. "They're filthy. God knows what awful diseases they carry."

"They need our help Julia; can't you see that? And it was to save them from disease that we brought them here."

"How dare you do this to me. We have hardly enough food for ourselves," she said savagely.

"Have you no compassion. Can't you see they need our help?" he said.

"Give them something to eat, and get rid of them." Going over to where her mother stood, Marcia stood directly in front of her.

"Mother," she began, "you are the most heartless, unfeeling human being. No one is asking you to soil your hands. I am the one who brought them here, and I will look after them."

"I am your mother Marcia. You have no right to speak to me in that tone. Now remove them to the kitchen. And I expect them to be gone by the morning." Putting the handkerchief back over her mouth and nose she walked past them and back into the drawing room.

"I am ashamed, to say that she is my mother," Marcia said, with a sigh, as she led them towards the kitchen.

Chapter 4

The Rectory

Cassie lay in bed in the strange room above the rectory kitchen wide awake listening to the rhythm of her mother's steady breathing. Her skin still tingled from the hard bristles of the brush, that Marcia had scrubbed her with in the tin bath in front of the fire. She passed a thin hand over the softness of the outsized night-shirt that covered her tingling body, and over the silkiness of her clean hair. Turning to face the window, the moon shone full into the room, filling it with shuddering light. It was beautiful, cold and false. It played tricks; turning the friendly tree that taps benevolent fingers at the window into a nameless horror scrabbling at the pane; making of an empty hearth an open grave and the round picture above it a window through which she may not look, for the fearful things it might disclose. Slipping out of bed she closed the curtains. But the curtains were thin and could not quite shut out the ghostly light. To burn a candle was unthinkable extravagance. But there was the little candle. Her father's candle, with a strange pain at her heart she lit it, and the warm colours shone softly out, familiar and reassuring. It was like her father himself, all warmth and friendliness and comfort. And the moonlight was like the woman who shouted, 'get them out of here. God knows what diseases they carry.' Then she thought of how different her daughter Marcia was; she was soft, kind and sympathetic. Then she remembered that she had no hunger pains tonight, and that tomorrow she wouldn't have to search for food, or sticks for the fire. This thought brought her comfort. Then blowing out the candle, she crept back into bed and slept.

When they awoke they lay silently listening to the sounds from the kitchen underneath them. The window faced east, and was soon filled with the yellow glow of the rising sun. Cassie's spirits rose, as she watched the warm glow fill the room, dispelling the ghosts of the night. Their cabin at home had no windows, because windows meant more rent, and so their days were spent in a twilight.

They heard footsteps on the stairs, and stiffened in fearful anticipation. Would it be the angry woman demanding their departure from the house? When the door was opened and they saw a smiling Marcia, their muscles relaxed.

"Good morning. How do you feel today?" she asked.

"Alright. A bit better." Cassie replied.

"When you are dressed, you can come down to the kitchen. Maggie will give you some porridge. Maggie is the cook. She's not so bad when you get to know her. I'm sorry about last night. I'm ashamed about the things my mother said to you." Then with a sigh, she added, "just try to keep out of her way."

Ellen cleared her throat, and said,

"I think it would be better all round, if we went to the workhouse. And in the spring we will go to America. The landlord is supposed to be paying the fare for them that is evicted, and destitute like us."

"Please don't go to that place. It would almost certainly take your life. I will look after you until you're both strong again. Then you can go to America if you wish."

"But we're not wanted here. And I don't want to be where we're not wanted. We have our pride; even if that's all we have left."

Marcia looked at the woman with the sad haunting eyes, and emaciated body as she lay on the bed, and was filled with admiration for her. Although penniless, and destitute she had an air of pride about her that left Marcia feeling humble in her presence. Then she asked,

"will you stay here, just until you are both stronger?"

Ellen nodded silently.

"Good. Now you can get dressed and I'll see that

you get some breakfast." She was about to leave the room when she noticed the small piles of dirty, threadbare rags that lay on the bedside chair. Then clearing her throat, she looked at Ellen again, and asked, "can you sew?"

"Aye, I can."

"And she can read and write, and speak in the Latin," Cassie added, with pride in her voice.

Marcia looked at them with a look of wide eyed surprise on her face, before asking, "who taught you?"

"Michael, my husband who was drowned. He was a teacher.... at times when he had pupils."

"I must tell my father. He is sure to think of some good use to put this to. But in the meantime we must get back to the business of altering clothes for you. My mother has a trunk full of clothing she won't wear again; they could be altered to fit you. You won't mind...er, someone else's cast off's?"

They both shook their heads simultaneously. Going over to the door she turned to face them again.

"Look, I'll bring you your food in here for today, until you get something to wear sorted out." Then she was gone leaving them alone with their thoughts. As she stared at the door that Marcia had closed behind her, Cassie thought it was a welcoming door, a hoping door and the worn wooden stairway that led to it, her ladder to new hope.

Marcia walked into her father's study carrying the clothing that she had found in the old trunk. Unaware of her presence, she observed her parents in the midst of a hostile row.

"I refuse to ask my family to support two penniless disease ridden peasants. I am ordering you to get them out of this house right now. To think that I could have married Jonathan Charles, and lived the life that I was born to live instead of a useless do gooder like you is beyond me."

"Please stop this Julia. Try to think of someone but yourself for a change."

"What kind of a life have I got here Henry, answer me that? "I have no company of my own kind. I have nothing in common with these miserable wretches that surround me."

"These miserable wretches, as you call them need our help." Then raising her hands to silence him, she yelled.

"You are not going to contaminate our son the way you have Marcia. She should be at a finishing school where she will meet her own kind; not running around miserable hovels with you. And if you must know.... I'm glad I got rid of that riffraff she was associating with."

"Don't make me despise you even more." Ignoring his comment she went on, "she must find a suitable husband, who will be able to afford to keep her in a proper lifestyle. God knows what will become of her.

But, Henry will not come under your influence of that, I'm sure."

"Poor Henry hates that school you have sent him to. In letter after letter he begs me to allow him to come home. But I suppose his happiness means nothing to you, so long as he mixes with the right kind of people."

As she watched, in that moment Marcia hated her mother so much that her hatred seemed to take shape and hang between them; a visible, tangible thing which seemed to consume her completely. Her hatred was so strong, it frightened her, fearing that the emotion would get out of control, that she might do something terrible to her. And so she walked away without being seen.

In the room above the kitchen, Cassie put on the dark blue frock that her mother had created from the old gowns that had lain in the trunk. As she looked at the skinny little figure in the ill-fitting frock, Marcia was filled with admiration for the dignity of the child before her. Cassie gave her a smile of gratitude, then going over to where Marcia stood, she put her arms around her waist.   "Thank you," she said softly. Lifting her up, Marcia pressed her head against her shoulder, and rocked her body gently as if she were an infant. In that moment Marcia vowed that she would care for this child, and somehow bring joy back into her young life.

Chapter 5

The Madam

In the kitchen Maggie greeted the newcomers with suspicion. She felt that her burden was heavy enough, struggling as she cooked for the family, with ever dwindling supplies of food. She was beginning to feel all of her sixty-four years; forty-five of which were spent in this same kitchen. The last eight years cooking for Julia Briggs, was without doubt the worst that she had, had to contend, with in all her years as a cook. She constantly complained about the food she prepared, never taking into account the scarceness, and poor quality of the raw materials provided. But, she knew only too well that she could send her packing at the least possible excuse. And, so she had to pander to her every whim, because the alternative was to be cast out penniless to starve, with no family of her own on whom, she could seek refuge. She busied herself around the range, stirring the porridge with aggressive strokes of the wrist. Without uttering a word, she put two bowls of the porridge on the table in front of them. When they had finished eating, Ellen got up from the table and went over to the range.

"I want you to know," she began, "that we won't stay here any longer than we have to. Thank you for the porridge." With that she walked towards the door. "Wait," Maggie said, coming up behind her.

"I'm sorry. I don't mean to be unfriendly. It's just that I have a lot on my plate, trying to run this place, with almost no help, and so little food to go around.

Lizzy Donnelly does the cleaning. She's deaf and dumb, poor creater. Aye, but there are times when I have said it's good for her. God, forgive me. But she can't hear the Madam's bad tongue nor hear the constant bells. Aye, being deaf has its compensations."

"I will help you in any way I can. And so will Cassie here," Ellen offered.

"That's good to know. But you need to rest, and to get a bit of meat back on your bones first." Then looking at Cassie, she said, "maybe you could find a few blackberries for me. I have hardly any preserves this year." Taking the basket she held out, Cassie made her way along the drive pleased to be of help in the ever present search for food. Her spirits were dampened, when she found that the blackberries were virtually non-existent, they had been picked by children from the village. Torn by the thorns, and stung repeatedly by the overgrown nettles, she walked on further afield hoping her luck might change. Rounding a bend in the lane, she saw a high grey stone wall that seemed to go on forever.

Walking slowly along it, she found a gap that was just big enough to squeeze through. She crept silently along the path through the trees, which led to a high walled garden. The path stopped at an iron gate above which flowed a riot of rambling roses. She peered through the gate cautiously, and saw two men with hoes in their hands toiling silently in the dark earth. As she watched, the elder man straightened his back, and looked up at the sky. "Dinner time," he said aloud, as they downed their hoes and walked towards the gate. Cassie scrambled back to the safety or a nearby tree, and watched as they crunched their way along the gravel path, and out of sight. When she was sure that it was safe, she went into the garden, and her eye was immediately drawn to the ripe black plums on the nearby trees. She hastily climbed up to where the fruit hung, and picked them at speed, flinging them to the ground. Climbing down again, she gathered them into the basket, and made a hasty retreat with her treasure.

In her haste she soon discovered that she had taken the wrong path, and was hopelessly lost. The path was flanked by, black, motionless monkey-puzzles, and then a clearing to a sloping green lawn leading to a large lake. Then her eyes moved upwards to the huge manor house, mellow and gracious, with mullioned windows, and roof of stone slates. In front of it was a paved terrace, which overlooked the lake, and the hills beyond. Cassie felt overwhelmed by the beauty and grandeur of the sight before her. She knew from her father's description, that, this was Albertine Hall, the home of Lord Charles Simms; the absent landlord. So transfixed was she on the sight before her, that the horsemen riding up the drive were almost on top of her before she spotted them. Just in time, she hid herself behind the monkey-puzzle, and watched them pass. She recognised, the front rider as John Brown, the land steward who had evicted them, and she shook uncontrollably, at the memory of it. From her hiding place she watched the riders disappear around the back of the house, before emerging from behind the tree. She ran quickly back along the path, and she thought how heavy her feet felt and yet made no noise, so that she seemed like a figure running in a dream.

Back again at the walled garden gate she quickly found the right path back to the hole in the wall, and back onto the laneway. Walking a little way, she sat down on the ditch to rest, while her heart still thundered in her ears. A pale rim of sun pressed against a solid grey sky in a hopeless effort to break through. Distant noises of human life were muted, beating against the consciousness without making proper contact; as in a nightmare one beats, slow abortive fists against a door, never actually touching it. Looking down at her basket of plums, she whispered "at least I have something to take back to Maggie."

It was almost dusk before she found herself back in the

rectory driveway, where she had the misfortune to run into Julia Briggs. Upon seeing the plums, she grabbed her by the shoulder, and asked,

"Where did you get those plums?"

"In a garden," Cassie answered, in a voice that was little more than a whisper.

"Where did you steal them? Tell me now where you stole them?" she screeched. Cassie fled from her towards the kitchen door in terror. Her foot caught on a stone at the edge of the driveway, sending her sprawling to the ground. Looking up, she saw Julia's damp face filled with hate, and she, too, seemed unreal; part of the dream into which she had fallen; a creature who had meaning but no substance. Seemingly, from nowhere Marcia was helping her to her feet. "Go away mother. Leave the wee child alone," she said, with menace in her voice.

"Do you realise, that.... little thief has been stealing plums in our name. God knows, I have but little pride left. But I will not have our names linked with thieving."

"Just go. Go away," she added.

As she walked back towards the house, Marcia picked up the scattered plums and put them back into the basket.

"Cassie. Where did you get the plums?" Marcia asked, as they reached the kitchen door.

"I'm.... not sure. It was a big garden with walls , near a big, big, house.. with a lake. I think it was the Hall."

"Yes, Cassie the only place round here that fits that description, is the Hall. But, God only knows how you got out of there without being spotted." Then getting down on her knees in front of Cassie, she said, "promise me that you will never go back there again. I don't care about the few plums. But I care about you. John Brown is the land steward; and he is a dangerous man with no mercy."

"He evicted us," Cassie said quietly.

"Is your head hurt?" Marcia asked, bending down to examine the bruise caused by the fall. "God knows how I'm going to tell your mother about this," she added with a sigh.

"It's all right. I'll just tell her I tripped getting the plums."

In the kitchen, Maggie looked at the basket of plums with pleasure. "How did you manage to get these?"

"In a deserted garden," Marcia fibbed.

"Well bless my soul. You did well, waine. You can help me to make some jam in the morning. I have some apples; plum and apple will do nicely. We have no sugar mind you. But I can use some of the honey that Brown gave the Madam."

Turning to the fire, she poured broth into a bowl, and put it on the table, "eat this, and then go and tell your mother that you're back safe. Aye, like I said, the honey will do nicely to sweeten the jam, even if I hate the swine that supplied it."

"Does he come here?" Cassie asked, with fear in her eyes.

"Aye, he comes here. Not to see the Reverend mind you, for he can't bear the sight of him. It's the Madam he comes to see. They say, that one of these dark nights someone, somewhere... will blow him into eternity. Aye, that's what they say. And in the meantime he brings honey for the Madam."

Lying on her bed, Ellen thought it a strange thing, the quietness that is born of shock. The hours go by. Dawn breaks and night falls. The robin cocks his head, chirping for crumbs on the window cill. Bread is baked and floors scoured, and life goes on. And a hand lies heavily on the heart numbing pain. When the hand lifts the pain will be there, it will have to be borne; but in the meantime there is the floor to be scoured, bread to be baked and a child to be fed...

Then the door opened and Cassie came in, and smiled at her.

"Are you all right?" she asked gently. As her green eyes, so like Michael's met hers, the heaviness lifted from her. And she held out her hand to greet her.

Chapter 6

The Visit

John Brown rode his horse along the laneway on his way to visit Mrs. Henry Briggs; ever watchful of what might lay in wait behind a ditch or tree. In many ways he was exhilarated, by the sense of danger that surrounded him.

He took little pleasure from Julia's company. What little humour she had ever possessed had turned to a sour habit of sarcasm. But, he had a plan in his head that would involve Julia, and might get himself even with the Reverend. He had been a thorn in his flesh almost from the moment he arrived in the parish, unlike his predecessor, who was content enough to do his religious duties, and relax with his port in the evenings. He still smarted with indignation at his latest form of attack. The Reverend had complained about his eviction of a mother and child at great lengths, and again about his responsibility for what had become of young McFarland. Then he produced a letter that he had written to Lord Simms. 'I never do anything behind backs,' he had said, 'so I want you to read this letter before I dispatch it to your employer.' In the letter he had complained bitterly about his handling of the estate. He had begged of him to return, and see for himself the misery, and hardship that his tenants were living in. John Brown's anger was so great, that he couldn't finish reading the letter. He doubted that his Lordship would take much notice of his complaints; but he could not be certain. He liked things the way they were; he had access to the Hall and treated it as his home, where he entertained, including girls that attracted his attention, which he could threaten or bribe to bend to his will. He wanted nothing to change. "He will regret poking his nose in my business," he muttered to himself. He had brooded on this incident for days, and now he was about to put his plan into action.

In Julia Briggs's, drawing room John Brown pretended to listen sympathetically to the endless complaints about her life. How she could have chosen from a dozen suitors, far superior to Henry; she could have been living in one of the Shires in luxury, with a town house in London. "And to make matters even worse, he and Marcia brought two starving, diseased ridden peasants into our midst."

"Where did he find them?"

"You might well ask. Marcia refused to let them enter the workhouse, in case they caught something, if you don't mind." She rolled her eyes heaven wards, in a gesture of helplessness. Reaching across, John Brown clasped her hand, in a mock show of attention.

"Dear, dear, lady, you have my deepest sympathy.

I have just thought of something that might bring a little cheer into your distressing life. I could arrange for you to spend an evening up at the Hall; send the carriage to collect you . And I could invite the Miss Bedford's, from Drimlin house. You could have a look around the house, and so on. What do you say?"

"Mr. Brown, how very kind and thoughtful you are. I do believe that I should enjoy that very much."

"Good! Say a week from today. The carriage will call at around seven."

"I'll be waiting. And thank you again."

Riding home through the dark laneways, John Brown was well pleased with his evening's work. The trap was set, the consequences of which was to be far reaching for all at the rectory. He slouched in the saddle, the reins slack in his hands, remembering the old crone of a fortune teller's words, "watch out 'and keep yer' wits about 'ye when abroad at night. For there lurks danger." He wished now that he had gone on about his business that day at the fair, and kept away from the gypsy. He lashed his horse across the rump with the whip, and galloped off into the gathering darkness.

From the room above the kitchen, Cassie watched him go with mixed emotions. She feared him, and yet she was glad in a way that he had evicted them, for she had grown to hate the misery of their lives in Glencullin, without her father to protect them. Memories of her father, in those now, seemingly far off summers as he taught in the hedgerows floated back. She could smell the sweet early summer grass, and the Hawthorne blossom. Suddenly she wanted to find her writing slate. She wanted to write all that she had learned in case time might erase it forever from her mind. Going over to the straw bag, she rummaged through it, almost frantically, until she found it. As she began to write with the small piece of chalk, she had a feeling that he was not far away, and that she was not really alone.

She wrote frantically, almost everything that she could remember until the chalk ran out. Marcia's voice startled her as she came into the room.

"What were you writing Cassie?" she asked, squatting down beside her.

"Just the things my Daddy taught me. But I have no more chalk."

"Listen Cassie. If I get you writing books will you promise me that you will write in them every day? That way you can keep a memory of everything that happens. You could start by writing down everything that you remember about your Daddy. I think that would make him happy, don't you?"

She nodded, a bright smile lighting up her small face. Then she asked, "could I write to Johnny too? I could tell him about you and his Mammy and Daddy,' and everything," she added, excitedly.

"All right Cassie. I'm sure he'd like that. Every wee bit of news from home is welcome, when; you're so far away. I'll go down now and find you a book to write in. And when that's finished I'll get you another one. But don't waste any space; paper is very expensive."

When she returned with the book and pencil, and showed her briefly how to keep a diary, she left her alone to write.

She wrote on, and on until darkness fell. At last spent and tired, she crept into bed and slept.

Marcia saw the small figure of Cassie, watching her from her window, as she was about to make her way to the shore. The lonely little figure tugged at her conscience, and so she returned to the house and asked her if she wanted to come with her. She nodded her head vigorously as a light of pleasure came into her green eyes. They walked hand, in hand towards the shore in silence until they reached the silent boathouse. Marcia stood silently by the locked door, and her heart felt heavy. 'Why do you keep hoping. You knew he wouldn't be here,' she silently told herself. For just an instant, through some queer trick of the imagination, it seemed to her that Johnny stood there in the doorway. And the quick ache brought tears springing into her eyes. The sudden squeeze of Cassie's hand reminded her that she was there.

"Why are you crying?" she asked, softly.

"Oh, it's a long story. I'm thinking about Johnny and how much I miss him. He was forced to go to Canada, because of me. Now I don't know if I'll ever see him again," she sighed.

Looking up at Marcia, Cassie said, "he'll build a big, big boat in Canada, and come back here to you." Looking down at her earnest small face, and the concern in her eyes, Marcia was deeply touched. Then, exactly what she had said caused her heart to race. 'Why didn't I think of that? Boat building is all he knows, and he is sure to find work in a boatyard.' She felt more hopeful now, about finding Johnny, than she had done at any time since his disappearance. Then smiling down at Cassie they walked along the shore path, to see Johnny's parents. As they went towards the door, Marcia was glad that they no longer, treated her with hostility. They sat silently at either side of the fire as usual. Clearing her throat loudly, Marcia said from the doorway,

"it's me. Marcia." Turning their heads to look at them, the old woman smiled, and got to her feet.

"Come in Marcia. Come in. And who is this waine?" she asked, peering at Cassie.

"This is wee Cassie O'Connor. Remember, I told you about the mother and child being evicted."

"Oh, aye, I heard that story, going around in the neighbourhood. Come up and sit by the fire. I have a wee bit of news."

"About Johnny?"

"It's not much. But it has lifted our hearts a wee bit. A few of the neighbours came on one of the redcoats in the town. One of them, that lifted Johnny. He was put on a ship bound for Saint John in Canada. Anyway, we since found out that it arrived safely, thank God. Mind you, they had to beat it out of him."

Marcia was filled with a new sense of hope as they made their way home in silence, hand in hand. They stopped momentarily at the boat shed. Memory was stronger than Marcia had bargained for; a sadder and at the same time a sweeter thing, more precious now and more poignant. The tide was creeping in quietly, putting out long impatient arms of rivulets that ran towards the land between ridges of sand. She felt Johnny's presence come closer as she watched the incoming tide, and was comforted.

When they reached the driveway, a carriage rushed passed them between the pillars, causing them to jump out of it's path. Marcia recognised the Hall crest as it passed.

"Did you see who was in the carriage?" she asked Cassie, with a puzzled frown.

"Aye it was your Mammy I think."

Marcia felt uneasy as they walked towards the house. This had to be John Brown's doing, and that her mother could befriend such a man filled her with resentment.

Julia Briggs stepped down from the carriage at the front steps of the Hall to be met by John Brown.

"Welcome, welcome dear lady," he said, sweetly offering her his arm as they made their way up the sweeping steps. Walking into the big hall he pulled the bell rope. A drably dressed woman with a sour expression appeared promptly. "Take the lady's coat, Mary," he ordered. Mary eyed Julia sullenly, taking her coat without uttering a word. As they went towards the dining room, Julia could sense her sullen eyes penetrating her, and she shuddered uneasily. When they were seated, John Brown cleared his throat, "I'm afraid the Miss Bedford's can't make it. It seems Jane caught a chill. But, we can have dinner alone, and still have a pleasant evening."

"But it may not be... er, seemly. Perhaps it would be best if I returned home after dinner."

"Nonsense Julia. And anyway it would be much too dark for the carriage to travel on the narrow roads." Getting up to his feet he took her hands in his and smiling down at her he said, "you will be perfectly safe with me."

Hearing a low cough, Julia turned around to see Mary scowling at her from the doorway, her head moving from side to side.

"The dinner is served Mr. Brown," she said loudly. She stood silently aside to let them pass, and as Julia went through the doorway, she reached out and pulled her sleeve roughly, nodding towards the dining hall.

"What is this woman trying to tell me?"

"Ignore her. She's a bit strange. Mad you know," he added, turning his index finger around the side of his head for emphasis.

The meal was served by a young, nervous girl with trembling hands, overseen by the ever watchful, suspicious gaze of Mary.

"You must try this wine. It's the best his Lordship's cellar can offer," John Brown coaxed, filling Julia's glass.

"Only a little. I seldom drink alcohol."

"It's a special occasion. And it is of the very best quality," he said, with a smile ignoring her protest.

Warmed and relaxed by the wine, and the grandeur of the surroundings, Julia talked incessantly throughout the meal. As she talked, John Brown refilled her glass with the wine which she drank with relish. When the meal was over, he went to the sideboard, and returned with two filled glasses. Because his back blocked her vision she couldn't see the small pouch of white powder that was added to one of the glasses.

"To our good health," he said, as he clicked his glass against Julia's.

Only when the port glass was empty, did Julia feel the room begin to spin.

"I'm.....afraid....I must...... retire," she slurred.

Julia Briggs awoke in daylight from a troubled sleep.

The room looked unfamiliar, and she could remember little of the previous evening. Movement from beside her made her turn to look to her right. It was then that she saw the naked body of John Brown lying next to her in the bed. She lay still for a moment, as the inexplicable horror crept into the silence of the room. She could remember the dinner of the night before, but the rest was a complete blank; a terrifying inexplicable blank. Suddenly from her throat came a loud scream.

"Get out. Get out. Get out," she screamed over and over, clutching the sheet under her chin. Getting out of bed slowly, John Brown turned to face her grinning with satisfaction,

"don't you even remember how much you enjoyed it? Eh?"

"You tricked me. You are an evil man, like Henry always said you were. Oh, God, Oh, God help me." Sobs shook her body and her head throbbed with pain. When the sobbing finally ceased, she lay rigid. A wave of cold ran down her spine, down her arms, and under the sheet she held tightly around her body, making her shake gently where she lay. 'I'm disgraced, ruined. I will never dare to show my head in the sunshine again,' she muttered in her torment.

Finally she summoned up the strength to get up and dressed. From the top stairway she peered down into the dimness of the big hallway, before making her decent.

She saw a figure pass before the faint and livid clearness of a doorway. Mary stood glowering at her from the study door in the distance.

"Is the carriage ready?" she asked, in as steady a voice as she could manage.

"The trap will do you he said. Jimmy will yoke the pony when he has his breakfast."

"Tell him to take the carriage. I can't be …seen in a trap," she stammered.

"It's the trap or you walk."

As they stared at each other across the space between them, Julia saw a mixture of pity and contempt in Mary's face. Quivers ran over Julia's broad cheeks, across the thin lips, ran across the wrinkles at the corners of her swollen eyes. She stammered…

"I demand the carriage. My eyes need shielding from the sun. I have a headache." Mary stared at her in silence for a few moments before saying quietly.

"I did try to warn you… for the Reverend's sake."

"I have no idea what you're talking about," Julia stammered. 'Dear Lord God, she knows, she knows.' she whispered silently to herself as she slumped down on a nearby chair.

As the trap made its way along the avenue, Julia sat stiffly with her head lowered. The pony trotted at a smart pace past the gate lodge and through the big ornate pillars, leaving the shade of the tall yew trees of the avenue behind them. The bright sunshine seemed to mock her, as she was seized with a furious hate for John Brown, but most of all for herself. During the remainder of the journey, she made plans for when she arrived home. 'I will tell them that I am ill. Headache; yes bad headache. That way I can draw the curtains and hide away in my shame,' she muttered silently to herself.

She stood at the front door of the rectory silently listening and watching, her whole being quivering with apprehension. She walked through the hallway on tiptoes and on upstairs silently to her room unobserved. Inside, she wandered aimlessly about the room, putting bottles on the bedside table, trying to fit with trembling hands the lids on the hat boxes. Whenever the real sense of what had happened emerged for a second from the haze of her thoughts she would fancy that something had exploded in her brain without, unfortunately, bursting her head to pieces, which would have been a relief. At last exhausted, she drew the curtains, undressed and fell into bed.

By evening she pulled the bell rope and waited. She could hear Maggie's slow lumbering frame as she made her way up the stairs for what seemed like an age, before she finally knocked on the door.

"I'm ill Maggie. It's my head. Tell the Master and Miss Julia that I don't want to be disturbed."

"Anything you want Madam?" Maggie asked, still panting from the exertion.

"A little broth perhaps."

"Is it all right if wee Cassie brings it up? I'm just not fit for them stairs no more."

"Very well. Now go; my head can stand no more."

Ellen was taking the bread from the oven, when the kitchen door opened.

Maggie slumped down on a chair in the kitchen to catch her breath;

"this is a turn up for the books. The Madam's ill she says. Wants broth in her room. And when I said I wasn't fit for the stairs no more, and could Cassie bring up the broth, she said, very well! And there was me expecting her to tell me to pack my bags, like she usually does."

Cassie stopped preparing the vegetables and a distraught look came into her eyes, at the mere thought of going to the Madam's room with broth. On seeing her troubled expression, Maggie said, "don't fear pet. The strange mood she's in, sure she'll hardly even notice you. It'll save my poor oul legs," she coaxed.

Ten minutes later Cassie made her way to Julia's room, bringing the broth on a tray. She knocked timidly on the door,

"come in," a faint voice echoed from inside. Cassie was surprised and relieved at her subdued, almost apologetic mood. She put the broth gently on the bedside table and hastily made her escape.

Henry Briggs was mystified by his wife's strange behaviour. Never before, in all the long years of their marriage had he experienced his wife behaving so strangely.

She complained of headaches, but refused to see a physician. Henry had a strong suspicion that; John Brown was in some way responsible. When he hinted at this possibility she became agitated; almost hysterical and so he dropped the matter, which only confirmed his suspicions. He had urged Marcia to visit her mother, even though relations were strained between them. However, he had to confess that life was far more peaceful and less strained while his wife remained isolated in her room.

Marcia met Cassie on the stairs struggling with two buckets of dirty bath water. She had heard the bell echoing from the kitchen almost constantly, followed by Cassie's light steps running up the stairs for days. Now seeing her struggling with the heavy buckets made her furious.

"Give me those buckets Cassie. They are far too heavy for you. Don't let her put on you like this."

"It's all right. They're not too heavy; honest," she protested, keeping a tight grip on the handles of the buckets.

"She doesn't shout at me no more. And she won't make us go, if I work for her. Please let me do it.... please."

Marcia was stunned by her words. Looking down at her anxious little face, she had no idea about how insecure she felt until this moment.

"Cassie," she began, "no one is going to make you leave here. You don't have to become my mother's slave to stay. I want you here. My father wants you here.
And as for Maggie, well, she's delighted with all the extra help not to mention the company. Now give me those buckets."

Marcia was consumed with rage as she went into her Mother's room. She found her lying on the sofa by the window, the half empty bath tub, in the middle of the floor.

"Marcia dear, how good of you to come and see me. I'm still far from well," she said, putting her right had to her forehead.

"I'm sorry you're not well. But, that is no reason to treat that poor wee child as your personal slave. She was brought here for protection, not slave labour. "When I told her this, she begged me to let her carry on being your slave. You won't make them leave if she does your bidding without complaint. She begged me to say nothing."

"But I have no one to look after me, Marcia. No one."

"Oh, stop it mother, for Gods sake. Do you ever think of anyone but yourself? This is the wee child you welcomed into the house so nicely. Remember? Disease ridden, get them out you said, while you protected yourself with your lace handkerchief. "

"Please Marcia. My poor head can't take this."

"I think your head would improve if you made an effort to do a little for yourself. And I'm sure that coming downstairs to join the land of the living would help a lot too."

"I can't Marcia. I can't face it."

"Can't face what mother? What are you afraid of? If I'm not mistaken that damned scourge of a Brown had something to do with this. And that's what father thinks too."

Julia turned her face away from her daughter's gaze and began twisting her handkerchief into knots.

"Nonsense dear, nonsense," she said hastily, but Marcia wasn't convinced.

"Getting back to the subject of wee Cassie O'Connor. She is a highly intelligent child, who has been well educated by her late father. I want to help her get into a school of some sort. I want her to have a future that is as far removed from the hunger and misery, that they have had up until now, as possible."

"Hum. What good will education be to her? No

doubt she will marry some ignorant peasant, and have swarms of children."

"I don't believe that the man Cassie will marry will be ignorant. And, won't the children she might have, be fortunate in their mother. I suppose you think that her future would be better catered for, as your unpaid slave."

"Marcia, if you can't come to visit your sick mother without all these recriminations. Please don't come at all."

"I will leave when you promise not to ring that damned bell every few minutes. And when you stop having that child running up and down, at your every beck and call."

"Very well. Now go and leave me in peace."

"I will remove the remainder of your dirty bath water myself," Marcia said. Julia was conscious of nothing now but to get her daughter out of the room. As if she saw this, Marcia maliciously lingered, struggling with the half empty bathtub trailing it onto the landing. Turning around from the doorway to face her again, Marcia said,

"I'm taking Cassie out for a walk. So don't ring the bell. And by the way, I will be answering your bells from now on."

Julia stared back at her daughter with a look of contempt, mixed with defeat before she closed the door and was gone.

A letter sat on the porclein dish on the hall table. Marcia, went over and glanced at it absently; MISS MARCIA BRIGGS, leapt out at her from the envelope and she knew instantly that it was from Johnny. Holding it tightly to her chest, she ran into the study to read it in private.

Chapter 7

Dark Fears

The handwriting was big and bold, just as she knew it would be, and each word etched on the paper was also now etched on her mind. 'He is well. He has a job in a shipyard. He loves me, he loves me still,' her heart sang. But following her initial elation, sadness also came to her. He would not return until he had earned money, to provide a future for her. 'I only want you. I care nothing for money,'she whispered to the emptiness. She thought of him, working long hours in grinding loneliness and her joy was tinged with sadness.

Half an hour later, she walked towards the shore, holding Cassie's hand firmly in hers. She felt as though she had been climbing and climbing for a long, weary time, through the darkness and bewilderment of a thick forest. And now, at last, she had reached the summit. It was not an easy path. But at least the darkness was gone; the sun shone; the wind blew in her face and she could see where she was going.

Cassie was overjoyed with Marcia's mood of optimism and skipped alongside her happily; almost as happy now as she had been when her father was alive she thought. She had formed a deep bond with Marcia and was at her happiest in her company; she was for Cassie, a protector from all that was fearful and insecure all around her. The painful memory of the time they spent, hungry and alone in the dark cottage, her mother lost to her in a silent world of her own came back again stealing the joy of the present. And then she was alone sitting on the floor again, with the black blowing branches against the sky and a dark smell of earth rising up all around and the clip-clop of horses hooves sounding sharp in the still air.

"What is it Cassie," Marcia asked, seeming to sense her gloom.

"Oh, I'm all right."

"Why are you looking so sorrowful then?"

"Please let me see to your mother. I like doing it. Honest. And she's always nice to me now. And Maggie's legs are bad."

"All right...all right. But we take it turn about. And I carry the heavy stuff. Is that a bargain?"

"That's a bargain," Cassie said, smiling up at her.

Johnny's parents were standing at the cottage door with an air of excitement when they arrived. Marcia knew instantly that they also had a letter from Johnny.

They spent a happy hour together reading the parts of their respective letters to each other, then walked home in the twilight.

Marcia met her father in the hallway on her return looking agitated.

"I need a word with you Marcia. In here," he said opening the study door.

"I have to go away for a week or so," he began "it's Harry. He hasn't been well, and I'm going over to bring him home."

"What's wrong with him? How did you find out?"

"I got a letter this morning from the school. It seems he won't eat and has become very thin. I was accused in the letter of ignoring the previous letter; of not bothering about my son's welfare."

"Well, did you ignore their first letter?"

"You know me better than that Marcia. I wasn't given the letter."

"Mother!"

He nodded silently, a look of bleak despair crossing his face.

"Did you ask her about it?"

"I tried. But what's the use. She accused me of tormenting her again."

He looked sad and defeated and Marcia's heart ached for him. Crossing the space between them, she put her arms around him,

"It'll be all right. He's probably just, homesick," she soothed, trying to hide her own deep fears.

"I hope you're right, Marcia. I only hope you're right." 'Poor wee, Henry. I have been so busy feeling sorry for myself, I neglected you,' an inner voice cried.

"I want you to do a few things for me Marcia. I won't be back in time for my Sunday duties. So, I want you to go over to the Reverend Bedford's in Glenscullion, and ask him if he could manage to fit the Sunday service in for me. I have a letter here for you to give him. You can take wee Cassie with you for company."

"I'll go in the morning."

"I knew I could rely on you," he said with a soft smile.

"I will see to everything this end. You just concentrate on getting Harry home safe."

"About your mother. Try not to hate her Marcia. She is your mother... in spite of everything." He sighed deeply before going on, "she says that you have been very hard on her. Says you have no sympathy for her illness."

"I wish she wasn't my mother. I try not to; but I hate her."

"Marcia. Believe me... when I say, she is more to be pitied than hated. You are above that Marcia. I am not asking you to love her; or even to like her. But please pray to God, that you won't continue to hate her." The look on his face made Marcia suspect that his plea was as much for himself as for her.

"For your sake I'll try. That's all I can promise."

He kissed her lightly on the forehead, and went out of the room.

The day dawned bright and cold, as Marcia yoked the pony for the journey to Glenscullion. Cassie's bright little face shone with excitement at the thought of their outing. Ellen came out the side door laden with blankets and food for the journey.

"The broth should keep warm for a couple of hours. If you put the jar at your feet it will keep them warm. And don't worry about your mother. I'll see to her."

"Thanks Ellen. But don't run to her beck and call all day," Marcia said, urging the pony forward. She stood and watched them until they disappeared out onto the lane. It helped her spirits to see Cassie smiling again, and she was full of gratitude for Marcia's kindness to her.

She walked back into the kitchen to the sound of the clanging bell.

"The Madam has started already," Maggie remarked.

"Aye, I'm in for a day of it; of that I'm sure."

As Ellen made her way up the stairs for the twentieth time, she wondered if there was never to be an end to Julia's demands, and there was hours to go, until nightfall. "Yes Madam?" she asked, yet again.

"You took long enough to answer this time," she answered hotly.

"The stairs are tiring Madam."

"Remember that you would be in the workhouse if it wasn't for my money. "I've decided to take a bath. And make sure the water's hot."

Ellen sat down heavily on the stairs, tears filling her eyes. She wished with all her heart that she had someplace of her own. Any wee shack that she could call her own. Memory jumped backward. She remembered as if it were yesterday the happy winter nights not so long ago, when she and Michael entertained their neighbours at their own fireside; the music, the storytelling, the laughter. She saw him so clearly now playing the fiddle, his strong face, his curling hair set in earnest concentration; her heart ached with longing. Then she heard Michael's voice in her head, 'courage has the extraordinary quality of being there if truly wanted' the voice seemed to say. Getting up she went downstairs to fetch the water. She met Lizzy in the hall, and the sympathetic look in her eyes gave her courage.

Marcia turned the pony into the rectory driveway. Reverend Bedford greeted them with friendliness, a broad smile on his big ruddy face.

"Come on into the drawing room. My sisters will be delighted to see you both."

"My father was called away to England. Harry is sick, and needs to be brought home. He wondered if you could manage to do his Sunday duties for him?" Marcia asked wishing to get the reason for the unexpected visit out of the way first.

"Of course, of course I will manage. Hope it's not too serious. Now come on in and see my sisters."

The two middle aged sisters sat close to a roaring fire engrossed in their needlework.

"I have two visitors for you," the Reverend announced as they went into the room.

"Oh, how lovely. Come and sit by the fire. You must stay for lunch."

"It's very kind of you. But we can't stay too long. We want to make it back before dark."

"Well you'll have time for something cold then, before you set out again.

"What a beautiful child Marcia. Who is she?"

"Oh, I'm sorry. This is wee Cassie O'Connor."

"Ah, sure now I remember. Your father told me all about it. Cruel. Cruel, that's what it is." Jane always did all the talking, Marcia remembered; not letting her younger sister Molly get a word in.

Later while they were eating, Molly made a determined effort to befriend Cassie.

At a glance Marcia could see that Cassie was enjoying the fuss that was being made of them.

70

"Come with me when you have finished eating, and we will see what wee treasures I can find for you," she said. When they had gone, Marcia asked,

"is your cold better Jane?"

"I didn't have a cold, dear."

"Oh, I thought I heard my mother saying that you couldn't go to the Hall because you had a cold."

"The Hall? I never go to the Hall."

"Oh. I.... must have miss heard," Marcia stammered in embarrassment. 'I might have known, she lied. She is a liar as well as everything else' Marcia thought. Just then Molly came back into the room with a happy smiling Cassie, clutching her treasures. Their return saved Marcia further embarrassment.

On the return journey Cassie talked excitedly about the kindness of Miss Bedford.

"And she is making me a new frock for Christmas, it's lovely red velvet. She measured me an' all." Cassie spent the remainder of the journey admiring the broach, necklace and other trinkets that she had been given, while Marcia's thoughts were in angry turmoil. She wished that she hadn't mentioned her mother telling her that the Reverend's sisters were at the Hall for dinner. She should have known that she lied. It all served to increase the mystery surrounding her mother's visit to the Hall, and her strange behaviour ever since. Then she looked at Cassie's happy little face and her mood lifted.

Two days later Cassie caught a chill and was confined to bed. Marcia and Ellen took turns to answer the constant jangle of bells from Julia Briggs' room. Marcia's patience was fast running out as her demands for attention grew. Finally, in exasperation, she decided to consult Doctor Higgins. She had suggested this to her mother on several occasions, "no, no Marcia I don't want a doctor," she would shriek in agitation. But, Marcia decided to ignore her protests, and call on him. And, besides Cassie's chill was also causing her concern and she could kill two birds with one stone, she decided.

"I'm going out for a wee while. I'll be back in an hour or so," she announced to Maggie and Ellen in the kitchen, then quickly went out before they had time to ask any questions.

Outside she saddled the pony, and got on her back despite the fat pony puffing indignantly at having her nose turned away from her stable. The wind was fresh and sharp on her face. Poised against the blue arch of the sky a hawk hung motionless. From some hidden farmyard came a cheerful clatter of wheels; and a voice cried " hup, hup!"...a horse whinnied and the pony tossed her mane and whinnied in reply. And in the silence she could have sworn she heard Johnny's voice cheerfully telling her, 'everything will be all right.'

The deserted cottages along the wayside were a constant reminder of the endless cycle of emigration that the past three years had caused. She sighed deeply at their loss. But, not even this could dampen her new found feelings of hope in the promise of the future.

Chapter 8

Echoes of The Past

The doctor listened sympathetically, as she voiced her concerns about her mother's headaches and wee Cassie's fever, and he promised to call the following morning. As she was about to leave, she turned to him again, and said,

"my mother's reaction to your visit will be hostile. In fact, I should warn you that she doesn't know that you are coming."

"Oh, don't worry about that. I'm well used to hostile patients at times," he said with a dismissive wave of the hand.

She rode home feeling well pleased with her afternoon's mission.

Doctor Higgins followed Marcia up the wide carpeted stairs. She knocked quietly on the door and waited until she heard a voice say,

"come in."

"I've brought Doctor Higgins to see you mother,"

she announced, when they were safely inside the room.

"I thought I told you I didn't want to see a Doctor. Please leave. There has been a mistake," she said coldly, half rising from her position on the couch.

"Now that I'm here I may as well have a look at you Mrs. Briggs. After all, you don't want to have to remain confined to this room for ever," he added, ignoring her protests as he advanced towards her.

"Please leave. Marcia will pay for her disobedience."

With an immense deliberation he walked closer to where she lay and slumped down heavily in the chair.

"Headaches, Marcia tells me," he said opening his big black bag. "Aye, nasty things headaches."

As she watched, it was only with immense control that she stopped herself from laughing out loud.

"Call me if you need me," she said, in as steady a voice as she could manage, before making her escape. In the hall she giggled aloud at the scene she had just witnessed. She has met her match in the bold Dr. Higgins, she thought with immense satisfaction.

Fifteen minutes later he ambled down the stairs to where Marcia waited in the hall.

"Come into the study. We can talk there. Well, what do you make of it all?" she asked, closing the door behind him.

"I'm honestly not sure. I can't find anything

organically wrong with your Mother to be honest. Has she been through any traumatic experiences recently?" he asked suddenly.

"Not that I know of. This all began after a visit to the Hall."

"I heard through the grapevine that Brown has befriended her. Do you think that he is behind this in some way?"

"I'm not sure."

"He's capable of it. Aye, a devious man. But, she's giving nothing away. I'll come back in a week if you want. But at the minute she is saying very little, and there's little I can do for her."

"You handled the situation well," Marcia said, with a grin.

His pale moon face loomed reproachfully at her, as he rubbed his waxed moustache, then his face lit up with a wicket grin.

"Next patient, " he said, making for the door.

Cassie lay rigid in her bed as they entered, her small feverish face looked pinched and drawn.

"This is Dr. Higgins, Cassie. "

After he had examined her, he turned to Marcia. "She's feverish. I'll give her a bottle. With good care she should recover alright in a few days." As he talked Cassie watched them with round fearful eyes, before asking, "will I have to go to the workhouse?"

"What made you ask a thing like that? Of course you won't go to the workhouse," Marcia replied, mystified by her question.

"But....you said people with the fever go there to die."

"Oh, Cassie. No pet. Listen, you've only got a wee chill. Put that nonsense out of your head." Going back over to her bed, Dr. Higgins smiled down at her, before saying,

"Marcia's right. It's only a chill. Take the medicine, and you'll be running about the place in a few days." Then with smiles of reassurance they left the room.

In the hall Marcia explained Cassie's beginnings, and why she feared the workhouse.

"Poor child," he said, sympathetically, "both yourself and your father will surely be blessed for your compassion," he added before leaving.

No sooner had she closed the hall door behind him, than she heard the bell jingle irritatingly, as she knew it would.

"I told you not to bring a doctor here," she began angrily, as soon as she opened the door, "but no, you had to disobey me as usual."

"It didn't do a lot of good I must admit. Because you wouldn't tell what's really troubling you. And so we all must go on suffering," Marcia sighed, "but I'm not sorry I tried," she added defiantly. "Now, wee Cassie's sick," she went on, "and so I'm your new servant."

Her mother stared at her, her breath now coming in laboured gasps, "get out get out of my sight," she screeched. Marcia left the room with a renewed sense of anger and hopelessness.

Cassie recovered quickly once her fears about the workhouse were put to rest. From her bedroom window she watched the black mountain of cloud creeping in from the sea, and the brilliant shaft of lightning that flickered over the heaving sea lit up the dark sky. Then her attention was drawn to the front of the house, as a cart made it's way towards the front steps. She watched the Reverend jump down from the front of the cart followed by a small fair haired boy. Suddenly he looked up, as if sensing that he was being observed. There was a look of sadness about him as he stood gazing fixedly at her, a pale shadow, set against the black mountain of cloud overhead. Another flash of lightning lit up the sky, followed by the crash and roar of the thunder. She jumped in spite of herself. When she looked again, he had disappeared inside the house and the cart was trundling out the driveway through the driving rain.

She saw him only rarely during the following weeks, through an opened door or wandering in a corridor. He would give her a shy smile if they met and walk on by.

Mid December brought cold east winds and for Cassie this meant lugging basket, after basket of turf to keep the fires going. The Madam's room was the most difficult, as she struggled with the endless, laden turf-baskets up the stairs. She had seen the Doctor in the house again; but Madam remained confined in her room.

One morning they awoke to find a thick layer of snow. As she was filling the turf basket a ball of snow hit her on the shoulder. Swinging around she spotted Harry grinning at her from the side of a hay stack nearby. "Stop it she yelled," as he pelted her again with a second snowball.

"You're wetting my coat."

"You can always put on a dry one," he said sulkily, annoyed that she didn't join in.

"This is the only one I've got. And anyhow, I've work to do." With that she carried on filling the turf basket. When she straightened up he was standing beside her with a look of disappointment about him.

"If I get you a dry coat… will you come and play in the snow?" he asked shyly.

"I've too much to do. All the fires to see to. And then there's the Madam…er, your mother. She'll be wanting her trays brought up."

"I don't see why you have to do it."

"'Cos, there's nobody else to do it."

"If I help you, will you come out and play with

me?"

She looked at his face and the pleading look that came into his eyes, and she nodded, "alright." With a smile of satisfaction, he grabbed the side of the basket and helped her carry the heavy turf to the Madam's room. Half an hour later, they were out under the ice blue sky, with the crisp snow beneath their feet. They walked along in a rather uncertain silence until they reached the top of the hill, where they began to slide down the steep incline on their bottoms, until Cassie slid out of control and ended up entangled in a hawthorn hedge at the bottom. "We need a sledge of some sort," Cassie shouted from the bottom. "I'll ask my father to make us one," he said, as he patiently untangled her from the stubborn thorns. She looked up at him and smiled in gratitude, and in that moment Harry felt that he had found a friend. That she was a girl, and that he had only had male playmates up until now, didn't seem to matter anymore.

In the days that followed they played in the snow, sliding down every available hill with the new sledge his father had made and in turn he helped her with her daily chores. She told him about her father, her mother, their eviction and rescue from the workhouse, and he told her about the misery of the boarding school he had escaped from. As Cassie told him about her fears for the future, the eyes that looked back at her were blue and clear and kind, and when he laughed they wrinkled up at the corners. She had found a friend in Harry Briggs when she least expected it.

Harry began to look forward to each new day for the first time in ages, and he felt healthier and happier as the painful memories of the boarding school and its cruelties began to fade. His mother had of late summonsed him more, and more. 'You must get back to school; now that you are well again dear. And, I wish that you wouldn't spend so much time in the company of Cassie. Still, you will make lots of new friends when you are back at boarding school, darling,' she would say in that voice of smothering affection, that he had grown to resent more and more. He would make an excuse to escape, and this would bring on her tears of self-pity, which left him feeling guilty.

But, then there was Cassie with her green eyes that sparkled when she laughed and reflected deep pain when she was sad . He liked the chuckling sound of her laughter, and the gap between her front teeth that flashed white in the sunlight.

This was to be a time of carefree joy for both of them; a time that would be etched on their memory forever.

Chapter 9

Debt of Honour

Henry Briggs sat in the dark cottage, smelling of turf smoke and old apples.

The air of sadness, and loneliness surrounding the elderly couple was very real, and he sensed their pain at parting with their children, one by precious one, to far off shores. And now they were threatened with eviction.

"They promised to send us money when they found work and got settled. But, Brown won't wait. "A week's all he'll give us," the woman said sadly, not taking her eyes from the smouldering embers of the fire.
Henry sighed deeply before saying,

"I'll go up and have a word with him. I'm making no promises. But I'll try."

He urged the pony through the gates and along the sweeping avenue towards the hall. He breathed a deep sigh of mingled exhaustion and anger, for he held out little hope of any mercy from John Brown.

He walked up the wide sweeping steps to the big

oak door, and pulled the bell.

Mary opened the door,

"hello Reverend. Did you come to see him?" she asked nodding back towards the big hallway.

"Is he here?"

"Aye. I'll tell him," she said, as she opened the door wider to let him pass. Then she opened the study door for him, and he heard her shuffling steps fade away into the distance.

A few minutes later he heard the brisk footsteps of John Brown approaching.

"Greetings Reverend. What an unexpected pleasure," he said with a mock bow of the head.

"I have no time for pleasantries Mr.Brown. So, I'll get straight to the point. I've just come from the McElroys. They tell me you have threatened to evict them. I am asking you, no telling you not to." They glowered at each other in mutual contempt, for what seemed like an eternity. Then John Brown's thin lips parted to reveal a leering, contemptuous grin.

"I have a job to do. And if the rent remains unpaid by next week, then out they must go."

"But, they won't last five minutes in the workhouse. They will get the rent in due course. Their family made that promise before they immigrated. Have you no compassion?" he asked in exasperation.

"Compassion doesn't come into it."

Henry Briggs stared at the man facing him, his face

red with rage.

"I will see to it that you get out of here. I will go to the newspapers....a Minister of the Government. But.... I will get you out of here."

"How is your dear wife, Reverend?"

"My wife is no concern of yours."

"Oh, but that's where you're wrong. I believe that she has taken to her bed...since that night...of our little liaison. It was the wine and the weakness of the flesh I suppose. Poor women she felt such guilt afterwards. Adultery is such a sinful thing to a clergyman's wife. I must confess, I felt some of that guilt myself. I even contemplated making a public confession in church, would you believe? Oh, and I'm sure that if it ever made its way to the Bishops ears...." He trailed off with a shake of his head and a sneering grin again formed on his thin lips. In that moment Henry was totally consumed with hatred; the like of which he had never known before. Quickly regaining his composure, he said,

"I already know. You are an evil man who, will stop at nothing." Then moving closer to him, he said in as slow and menacing a tone as he could manage, "your day will come Brown. And it won't be too far into the future." With that he swung around and left the room. He was untying the pony in the back yard when he heard the faint click of a latch. Turning around he saw Mary staring at him and beckoning him towards an empty stable to the right. He followed her inside.

"Reverend, it wasn't the fault of your misses. He put laudanum in her wine. Aye, I seen it with me own eyes. I'm not telling you this for her, for she deserved all she got. No, it's for you. You're a good man, aye, a good man." Hearing a sound from outside, a look of terror crossed her face, and she bolted back towards the house without another word.

The pony walked slowly along the narrow coast road, and in the trap Henry Briggs sat lost in his own turmoil. He considered confronting her with what Brown had told him, or he could simply tell her that it wasn't her fault, like Mary had said. But, he knew that this would mean the return of the old demanding, and often cruel woman that in his honest moments he had grown to detest. He liked things well enough the way they were right now. He was free to sit alone and read, smoke his pipe, or do whatever he wished in his leisure without fear of Julia's constant criticism. He made his duty visits twice daily, and then blessed freedom.

He stopped the pony half way up the bray, and sat motionless contemplating the landscape. The dusk came from the hills, flowed over the coast, putting out the red fires of sunset, and went out seaward, pursuing the retiring tide. The wind dropped with the sun and the clouded sky descended low upon the black contour of the hill. The dead leaves danced in spiral whirls under naked trees, until the wind laid them to rest. He felt calm again, as he watched the powerful beauty all around, and at last, knew what he must do.

When he had fed and bedded the pony for the night, he went into the house, and settled himself down in front of the fire. Ellen brought his supper on a tray and when he had eaten it, he took off his shoes and lit his pipe and felt more at peace than he had done in a long time. He was lost in thought when Ellen came back to collect his tray.

"Thank you Ellen. How are you by the way? I have been very neglectful of late," he said, with a sympathetic smile.

"I'm not so bad, Reverend. Lonely at times."

"Are you content here?"

"Content enough, I suppose. But, I miss Michael, and my own wee place. Oh, but don't think I'm not grateful to you. For I am. Very grateful."

"Ellen, I know that you do a lot of work here. Maggie's getting old and couldn't manage without you. But we have taken you too much for granted. You would need to be paid for your work. And you're right; you do need a place of your own."

"Maybe I shouldn't have spoke. You have enough bothers. And wee Cassie is very happy here. Marcia has been so good to her... to both of us."

"I'm glad you have spoken. I'll give it a bit of thought and we'll come up with something, eh," he added with a smile.

As she made her way back to the kitchen, she decided not to mention her conversation with the Reverend to Cassie for the time being. She knew that she would react badly to any mention of leaving the rectory, and this caused Ellen some unease. But, in her heart she was glad, she wanted someplace to call her own again; some hope of being her own person again. She feared ending up like Maggie; old and feeble and homeless. She knew that the Reverend was an honourable man, but she also knew that if anything should happen to him in the future, she, like Maggie would become homeless. The thought of having somewhere to call her own again gave her heart a quick beat of pleasure.

Henry Briggs finished his breakfast and made his way upstairs to his wife's room. He found her lying on the long couch by the window as usual.

"Good morning Henry," she greeted him, without conviction.

"Good morning to you," he answered, seating himself on the chair facing her.

"I visited your friend Mr. Brown yesterday. It was on an urgent matter. He is about to evict an elderly couple whose entire family were forced to emigrate."

"Oh, Henry," she interrupted, with a sigh, putting her handkerchief over her eyes, "you know how I hate to be told these tales of woe."

Leaning over he snatched the handkerchief from her eyes, and in a stern loud voice he went on,

"this time you will listen to me." Ignoring the startled look of shock on her face, he continued in a softer tone, "as I was saying he is about to evict the old couple. I tried threatening him as usual, to save them from the workhouse. But this time he had one over on me my dear. Your little secret is out. He took the greatest pleasure in telling me all about it... every sordid detail. The wine and weakness of the flesh was his excuse. What's yours, I wonder, eh?" Grabbing the blanket that covered her legs, she hid her face in its folds, as small muffled squeaks of anguish came from her throat. Snatching the blanket from her face, he again forced her to look at him before going on, "he told me he was contemplating making a public confession for his sin. In church." Her eyes widened in horror as she listened, her mouth opening and closing with no sound coming out. "Oh, and he threatened me with telling the Bishop," he added. Turning her head away from his gaze, she began to cry.

"I'm sorry Henry. That evil man tricked me. But, I have made my peace with God."

"That's good to hear. Now, as I was saying, the old couple need twelve guineas to pay their rent. A fortune to them, but not to you.... eh?"

Getting up from the couch, she went over to a drawer. Then taking a key from around her neck she unlocked a wooden box. Returning to where Henry sat, she handed him a small pouch,

"there are two extra guineas in it," she said, absently.

"Thank you. They will much appreciate your kind gesture, as will the Almighty."

With a sudden jerk of the wrist, she grabbed his arm, "please, please don't talk of this to Marcia or Harry..... please. If they ever found out I'd die of despair."

"As you have been generous to the McElroys; sparing them the workhouse, I'll agree to that." With that he got up and left the room without glancing at her again.

As he went downstairs he felt small twinges of guilt at, not having told her about the laudanum. But, as his thoughts went back to the sad old couple threatened with eviction, the guilt left him like summer mist that burned away with the warm sun. He patted his pocket containing the money, as a wee smile formed on his lips.

Chapter 10

Repent Alone

Julia Briggs spent days alone in her room in a state of anxiety about the future. Her secret was out, and she could no longer bend Henry to her will; she had lost her grip on him. She could visualise him coming to her demanding money for every lame dog in the parish. 'I can't bear it…. I can't bear it,' she repeatedly whispered to the emptiness. Then she thought of a plan. Marcia was lost to her. But, she would not lose Harry. She would leave and go to her sister in Bath, using her health as the excuse. She must take the waters, and Harry must go with her.

She wrote the letter to Edith and pulled the bell rope. When Cassie answered she handed her the letter; "this must be posted today. You can walk to the village and be back before nightfall. And, when you go downstairs, send Harry up to me. Tell him I need to see him at once."

When Harry came in she greeted him warmly.

"I have the most wonderful plan for you and I. We will go to Bath to see your aunt, Edith. I will stay for a

few months until I get you settled in a nice new school."
Harry looked at her with fear in his face.

"No. No. I won't go. I will never go to England to a school again," he shouted, jumping to his feet.

"You will do as I say. You are a ten year old child, who will do what he's told."

Her face was now close to his, and she stared at him until her eyes seemed to become glowing coals that burned deep into his brain, and yet he was in mortal fear of making out the well known features. He could hear his breath coming in short gasps. Taking a deep breath he said as loudly and as defiantly as he could,

"I --won't---go ----with-----YOU. I will die first."

"I'm your mother. And I say that you will do exactly what you're told."

"I'll die first," he yelled again, "I hate you." Then he ran out the door banging it behind him. In the kitchen Ellen told him that Cassie had gone to the village with an urgent letter. He ran down the lane as fast as his legs could carry him, but she was nowhere in sight. He stopped for a few seconds to catch his breath, and began to run at a slower pace. He had to see Cassie. He must tell her how frightened he was. "I must catch up with her. I must. I must," he panted, as the terror took over again. At last exhausted, he sat down under the bare branches of an oak tree to await Cassie's return.

At last he saw her coming in the distance, and ran to meet her. As they drew level he could find no voice. He opened his mouth but no sound came.

"What's wrong? What's happened?"

"It's.... her.... my Mother. She's trying to force me back to a school in England. Says she's going too." He threw himself down and burst into tears, tearing angrily at the grass with his one hand. Cassie sat down by his side, not daring to touch him, not daring to speak. She began to cry, too. They lay side by side hidden by the gorse and cried together in the swift, black, annihilating despair of childhood, which lasts so short a time, but while it lasts sees no break in the clouds, or no hopeful ray in the sun. They lay and cried until they could cry no more. Then Cassie turned and gave Harry a watery smile, and put her hand in his,

"she can't make you go. She can't. The Reverend wouldn't let her take you away again," she went on, and then she kissed him on the forehead, pulling him to his feet.

"You will always be my very best friend," he said in a muffled tone, and the tear-filled eyes that met hers held a look of total adoration. "I'll talk to my father tonight," he added, suddenly cheerful again.

"Cry if you have to Harry. But make sure that she doesn't take you away." Then looking at him again, she said shyly, "you're my best friend too."

His father was bent over the desk writing his Christmas sermon, when he went into the study. Clearing his throat loudly, he asked,

"Can I talk to you father?"

"Come in Harry. What's troubling you?" he asked, noting his puffed, eyes, and a look of anxiety on his face.

"It's mother," he began, "she says I have to go to school in England again with her. I can't go back there. I won't." His voice trembled and his legs shook, as he stared back at his father. His mother always seemed to get her way in the past, he remembered. And as he looked at his father's puzzled frown, he could only fear the worst.

"You say your mother told you she is going to England?

"To auntie Edith."

"Well that's news to me. No, Harry, you don't have to go with her."

"But she said she'd make me go," he said in a half sob, suddenly remembering Cassie's advice.

"Have no fear son; she won't be taking you anywhere. You have my word on that." There was a determined tone in his voice, that Harry had never heard before, and he began to feel reassured at last.

"About school Harry," his father began again, "you will have to get into a new school after Christmas. I am enrolled you in a school up in Derry." Noticing the alarm in his son's face, he put up his hand before going on, "Derry's not far away, and you'll be home every turnabout."

But, Harry was troubled by the mere thought of another boarding school. A sudden emptiness came into the pit of his stomach. As if sensing his thoughts, his father said,

"If you are unhappy in the new school like you were before, I will take you back home. And I know that you have become friends with Cassie. But, she will have to go to school too." His face lit up and asked,

"can she come to the Derry school with me?"

"Afraid not son. Your school is boys only. But, Marcia will take Cassie up to visit you an odd time. And, you will have all the holidays to play together."

He considered this information for a few seconds, and nodded his head solemnly. As he looked at his young son, Henry thought how vulnerable and unsure he looked and reached down to put his had on his head.

"I'll always be here for you son. And don't worry about your mother. I'll talk to her later. Now, cheer up and smile." Looking up into his kindly craggy face, Harry felt a surge of happiness sweep over him, and he smiled a smile of affection for this big kindly man, who was his father. "That's more like it. And, by the way Christmas will soon be here. How about yourself and Cassie getting some holly and mistletoe; cheer the place up a bit for then." Harry grinned broadly, and ran off to find an anxious Cassie in the kitchen.

Julia was seated in front of the mirror brushing her hair when Henry opened the door.

"How are we this evening?" he asked.

"You could knock first," she answered sourly.

Ignoring her comment, he went on,

"I have spent the past half hour with Harry. What do you think you're doing, threatening the wee lad with nonsense about taking him to a school in England?"

"It's not nonsense. That is what I intend doing."

"No Julia. Harry is never going back there to school. I have enrolled him in an excellent school in Derry. And, let that be an end to it."

Julia's face reddened, and her eyes narrowed,

"you... you. How dare you tell me what's best, for my own son," she shrieked.

"I will, and I am, telling you what's best for our son. That is the end of the matter," he added, getting to his feet.

"How dare you walk away from me. Harry will not grow up like Marcia. He will have the education I want him to have. He will mix with the right people."

Turning around to face her again, he said,

"yes. Harry will have a good education. And yes he will mix with the right people. All of God's people."

He left the room, closing the door quietly behind him. Alone, Julia knew that she had lost this battle. The moment he had found out about her night of shame with John Brown, she had lost her hold over him. But she would find a way to get her own back.

"I won't let you win Henry Briggs. My day will come again," she vowed to her reflection..

Cassie and Harry skipped gleefully into the glen in search of holly, the echo of their voices ringing through the quiet valley. They were all too conscious, that their carefree days were fast coming to an end. It was easy for Cassie to imagine   Harry's, new college with its crowded classrooms, its throngs of book laden students, its din of masculine voices; tramp of hurrying feet, and wished with all her heart that she too could be part of it. For his part, he wanted only to stay here with Cassie forever. They gathered the prickly holly with the greatest number of red berries, and tied it together to carry home. They sang all the Christmas songs that they knew as they made their way back up the steep path, and out of the glen. At the top, they sat down to rest, with the steep gorge, below and the gushing sound of the river over the steep rocks.

"I wish I didn't have to go away to that old school," Harry said suddenly.

"An' I wish that I could go with you. I would like a big school. If I was a boy maybe I could go too," she added wishfully.

"You must be mad wanting to go to school. They're horrible, awful places."

"Still, I'd like to go," Cassie persisted.

"If you seen one you'd see what I mean."

"Maybe Marcia would take me to see your school."

"Aye, an' you could dress as a boy an' stay instead of me. Then I'd stow away on the steamer back here."

"You're a lunatic," she said, with a grin pulling him to his feet,

"come on. It'll soon be dark."

They reached the house just before dark, and immediately set about decorating it with the holly and mistletoe. When they had finished they drank hot spiced milk by the flickering firelight, until their eyes grew heavy with sleep. Cassie knew that this would be a special day that she would always hold treasured memories of.

Chapter 11

Christmas

Cassie awoke on Christmas morning with mixed feelings. It had been arranged that the Reverend would give them a lift in the trap, to Mass at their old church in Glenscullion. Her father wouldn't be there anymore, and her memories of fear and hunger were still very strong. Still, her mother was set on going back and so she must follow.

She got up and dressed herself, and began pacing around the garden restlessly. The brown spaniel coaxed her to play, smacking a fallen leaf and leaping from behind a bush in excited capers, but she couldn't even smile. She could feel her eyes fill up with tears and fall silently down her face.

Marcia found her like that, and led her back inside the hall.

"What is it Cassie? I've been looking everywhere for you. I've got something for you. But, you're not getting it until you tell me why you're crying." Taking out her handkerchief, Marcia wiped the tears from her face. "Now, out with it."

"I don't want to go back to Glenscullion. My

Daddy's gone. An.... an' it was horrible when we were hungry, an' Mammy couldn't speak." Gathering her into her arms Marcia rocked her small body gently,

" it's all right Cassie. Sure you're only going to the church there and coming home again. And we have a goose for dinner. And I have a lovely present for you from Miss Bedford. Come on open it," she coaxed, handing her the parcel. The smile on her face broadened when she saw the velvet dress in all it's, glory, "I had forgoten all about it."

"Why don't you put it on now?"

"Can I?" she asked, her face lighting up. Marcia nodded, and she ran off excitedly to her room to put on the new frock. She reappeared a few minutes later smiling broadly, dressed in the new frock.

"It's lovely Cassie. Just a perfect fit. And, I have another present for you. But not 'till after dinner."

The day was blustery and dry as they set off for church. The Reverend was doing duty for Reverend Bedford as well as his own church and was able to give Cassie and Ellen a lift all the way to Glenscullion church. As they neared their old home, they discovered that memory was stronger than they had bargained for, more poignant and more painful.

Inside the church they recognised some of their old neighbours. But so many were gone. Death and immigration had taken a heavy toll over the past five years.

After the Mass ended Johnny Molloy came over to greet them, "good to see you both looking so well. I was so glad to hear that you avoided the workhouse. So many of our old neighbours have gone. America has taken all our youth."

Ellen shivered as she watched the huddled figures around the graves, and wished that she could at least visit Michael's grave. As she stood looking at the church, she remembered their wedding day as if it were yesterday. The pain was joy, and the joy was pain; it was all mixed up in her heart. Taking Cassie by the hand they bid farewell to Johnny and their old neighbours and walked away, as tears slid down her face.

The trap met them at the bottom of the brae, and moved off at a spanking trot towards home. As they neared the top of the hill, Henry stopped to rest the pony. He sat with knitted brows, gazing out at the rough white capped seas far below, before saying,

"it must have been hard on you going back today."

"Aye, it was hard. I envied the people with graves to go to." Then following his gaze out to sea, she said with a long sigh, "he's out there somewhere."

"Only his mortal remains, Ellen. Only his mortal remains. But, I know that having a grave to visit is a comfort. The sea is a hard master. You know, I was just thinking that it was about this time two years ago in forty eight that a hundred and seventy five souls were suffocated on the 'SS Londonderry' just off that headland. Aye, poor souls were trying to escape the famine. And instead through sheer neglect and stupidity they were deliberately imprisoned in a far too small space, in a rough sea, like it is now. "

"What happened to them responsible?" Cassie asked

"Oh, there was an inquest above in Derry. But, they were exonerated," he added with a sigh. Then, turning to face them he smiled, "don't let's be too sad. It's Christmas day; a time of new, hope. Let's get home to the goose, eh?"

The whole house was scented with the delicious aroma of the goose, when they arrived back. The dining room table had been set, and the fire blazed brightly.

"We are all eating together," Harry announced cheerfully, "and I have a present for you afterwards."
Looking at him with her big green eyes in her tiny face, Cassie said,

"I've got one for you too. It's only a wee present, mind you." He smiled back at her, as they ran off towards the kitchen.

They were about to sit down to eat, when Julia made her entrance, while each in turn looked on in stunned silence.

"Glad you decided to join us," the Reverend said, breaking the embarrassed silence.

"Happy Christmas Madam," Ellen and Maggie said, almost in unison. She made no reply, and sat down grim faced and unsmiling. During the meal she shot an occasional resentful glance towards her husband, who ate in a strained silence.

'She has spoiled everything,' Cassie cried out silently. 'Why didn't she stay in her room?' Then she stole a glance at Harry, and he smiled at her; a smile that lifted her heart from the gloom around her.

"Cassie," Julia's voice shrilled, making her jump, "go and make sure the kettle is boiling. I'll take my tea back in my room."

"Not until, you've finished eating Cassie," the Reverend's voice broke in.

Getting up from the table, scraping the legs of the chair on the wooden floor, Julia Briggs stood gazing down at her husband with hatred in her eyes. She stammered,

"I will thank you not to undermine my instructions. I want the tea right away Cassie," she ordered, starting out of the room in great haste, banging the door behind her.

Clearing his throat, Henry said pleasantly,

"I propose that Marcia, Harry and myself clear away the dishes when we have all finished eating. Then we will all meet in an hour or so in the drawing room for a few games, and perhaps a bit of singing."

The mood was suddenly lifted and the strain of the previous half hour or so gone, as everyone began to talk again.

That Christmas afternoon was one that Cassie was to remember for the rest of her life. Marcia's gift was a new coat and hat, the like of which she had never hoped to own. Harry gave her a pair of stout black boots.

"Marcia said these are what you needed most. I wanted to get you a catapult," he hastily added. Then handing him her parcel, she said,

"Marcia told me that this is what you needed most. I made it myself." He gave her a broad smile of approval when he unwrapped the brown scarf and socks that she had knitted for him.

Later, Harry offered to teach her how to play chess; and they played until sleep overtook them.

Chapter 12

Spring

In early March Harry came into the kitchen one evening with a sorrowful expression on his face.

"I have to go to the new school tomorrow."

The words had been more terrible, uttered in Harry's sad, broken tones. In spite of herself, Cassie felt hot tears spring into her eyes. He had become her best friend, the one whom she could tell her troubles to. And, now, she felt a deep sadness that went right down to the pit of her stomach. Pained by her tears, he said,

"I will be back again by June. And we will have the whole summer to play. And, you will be going to the school in Glenscullion next week too." She smiled a weak smile, through her tears,

"aye, you're right. Let's go out and play on the hill."

At the top of the hill they sat down together on the heather. They spoke very little. It was happiness enough just to be together in the silence and the warm, friendly smell of the moor.

"You will make new friends at the college," Cassie said, breaking the silence.

"So will you." He looked down at her and smiled, trying hard to mask his doubts, "but, you will always be my best friend," he added.

The following morning Cassie watched him get into the trap from her bedroom window. Tears leapt from her eyes and ran down on to the sill, and she weakly let them fall, despite promising him that she wouldn't weep at his going. He looked up at her for a fleeting moment with a wishful, longing expression.

When the sound of the trap wheels faded into the distance, she threw herself down on her bed and sobbed until her head throbbed.

Sometime later, she became aware of Marcia's presence.

"Don't cry anymore Cassie. I know that you will miss each other. But, sure he's only up in Derry. And, he'll be back in June. He would normally get home for Easter. But, it's not allowed because it's his first term. Anyhow," she went on, "you and I will go to see him around Easter time. We'll go up the Foyle on the steamer."

Lifting her head from the pillow, Cassie gave her a watery smile.

"Thanks Marcia. How many weeks is it to Easter?"

she asked, counting her fingers, "an' I've never been on a steamer before, or been to Derry." She felt excitement mounting, her grief momentarily forgotten.

As the days passed, Cassie found the pain of missing Harry begin to ease. They wrote to each other regularly, and although she still missed him greatly her loneliness, began to lessen. She began her first term at the village school two weeks after Harry's departure. It all seemed strange at first, but as the days passed she began to throw herself into the business of learning. Chores and homework took up most of her evenings, leaving little time to brood.

As March passed ragged fields were transformed into striped, chocolate Coloured squares and gulls flew inland to follow the plough in a slow, white wake. Young life staggered in the hedgerows, and the bright yellow gorse blossom glimmered in the sunlight.

At last Easter Monday came. Wearing the coat and hat she had been given for Christmas, she set off with Marcia for Derry. The pier at Moville was a hub of activity when they arrived to await the steamer. Groups of people stood silently huddled together, with tear stained, sad expressions as they awaited the boat that would take them out to the ship anchored off the shore, bearing them to America. A fiddler played a lament, the strains, seemed, to mirror the heavy air of sadness around them. As the boat came closer to the dock an old man ran out of the sidelines until he reached the young woman closest to the short gangway. They embraced silently for a long time, until she dragged herself away and got into the waiting boat. They watched from the now silent pier as the boat laden with passengers made its way out towards the waiting ship.

Cassie was relieved when the Derry steamer arrived to take them away from the sadness of the immigrants.

The journey up river was a joy to Cassie, as she ran from one side of the boat to the other scared to miss any of the sights along the way. The boat made slow steady progress around the gentle curves of the Lough, until at last the city came into sight. To Cassie's eyes the sight was magnificent. She had never been further than Glenscullion before and the sheer size of the buildings made her stare in awe.

Taking her by the hand as they left the boat, Marcia said,

"it's only a wee walk to the college. The Matron might find us a bed for the night, as most of the boys will be away." Looking up at her Cassie felt a strong surge of affection rush through her. And remembering the sad plight of the people leaving from the pier, she thought that had it not been for Marcia she and her mother would have been among them had they survived the workhouse. She loved Marcia with all the force of her sensitive child nature.

Seated on the steps of the college, Harry spotted their coming and ran to greet them. To Cassie he somehow, seemed more grown up in the weeks since she last saw him.

He took great pleasure in showing them around the empty classrooms while talking incessantly about their use and the teachers who taught there.

At the boarding house the matron appeared at the head of the stairs. Clad in decent black from head to foot, a shiny reticule clutched between cotton gloved hands, she stalked down the stairs into the hallway to meet them. The very sight of her sent Cassie diving for cover behind Marcia's back.

"You must be Marcia. I've heard all about you. And the wee person hiding behind you is Cassie, I believe."

Going around behind Marcia she looked down at Cassie,

"you can come out now. I don't bite at all." Looking up at her fearfully, Cassie was surprised to see a smile on the grim face, "I have something for you to eat upstairs, if you will follow me."

They followed her up the stairway and along a dark corridor, where she opened a door on the right. Inside the room a table was set and a turf fire smouldered in the grate. When they were seated at the table Cassie glanced nervously at the Matron, her face looked sharp as a skull in the dull light of the gloomy room. Glancing quickly at Harry, she smiled a smile of sympathy, and shuddered inwardly at the mere thought at having a black clad witch like the Matron in charge of him. Glancing at her again she thought, 'why, she looks even more frightening than the Madam.'

"Cassie," she said, in a voice as rusty as hinges, "do you want milk or tea?" Cassie jumped visibly, so tense were her nerves,

"ah, ...tea. Please," she stammered.

"Why, Cassie I think you're feared of me," she added, with a hint of a smile on her thin lips. Glancing at Harry again, she saw that he was grinning broadly. She felt her face blush red in embarrassment, and wanted to run out of the room as fast as her legs could carry her. Marcia's voice broke the awkward silence,

"is it all right if we take Harry out for a few hours Matron?"

"Aye, providing you have him back before dark."

When the meal was eaten, they thanked her kindly and went out into the spring sunshine. They walked around the stout city walls, admired the shops and walked along the quay were the big boats were anchored. After spending the night in Derry they bid a sad farewell to Harry and caught the one o'clock steamer back down the

Foyle.

As they waited for the mail car to take them on to Glenscullion, two men stood a few feet away. They couldn't help overhearing their conversation.

"The police are out in force," one of them said, "questioning everybody in sight, I hear. But they'll get nothing out of nobody. Aye, Brown won't be missed. He was a bad article. Shot him clean through the head they say."

Marcia and Cassie looked at each other in disbelief, as they listened to the conversation, trying to digest what was being said. 'Brown is dead,' Brown is dead' Marcia repeated to herself silently, and she couldn't help feeling glad. Cassie's memory ran back to the dark kitchen and John Brown's fearful threats. She found it hard to believe that it was less than a year ago, and that the seemingly indestructible, arrogant man was no longer in their mist.

Chapter 13

The Inevitable Hour

As the mail car made its slow bumpy way along the long stretch of coast road Marcia thought of Johnny again. The pain of his going had been re-enacted for her at the pier the day before, when she watched the sad farewell of the emigrants.

Now the man responsible was dead. The words of her favourite poem came into her mind.

> *The boast of heraldry, the pomp of power,*
> *And all the beauty, all the wealth e'er gave,*
> *Await alike the inevitable hour.*
> *The paths of glory lead but to the grave.*

Henry Briggs sat in the trap at the crossroads waiting for the mail car, his thoughts on the murder of John Brown. He couldn't help feeling a sense of relief at his passing, a relief that was tinged with guilt because it was in total contradiction to his Christian principles. And, yet, his whole being was elated with a sense of having been relieved from a great burden, however confused his reasoning might be at this moment.

He saw the mail car coming around the bend of the hill; a dark shape moving slowly, surely against the yellow evening sky. He sat very still and listened to the silence. He lifted his face to the darkening sky above the hill, where stars shone palely. There was no sound at all, save the horse's hooves, and the trundle of the mail car, coming nearer, and nearer. He gave himself to the silence, and knew God. Helping Marcia down from the cart, he asked,

"Did you hear about the shooting?"

"Aye, we heard. And I can only feel glad. Have you told mother?" He shook his head.

"She's the only one that will be sorry," Marcia said.

"Not even she will be sorry."

Henry Briggs gave Julia the news of John Brown's death the following morning. She stared into space without uttering a sound.

"Just thought I'd let you know," he said turning to go.

"I'm going over to my sister in England next week. Could you make the arrangements?" she said absently.

"If that's what you wish."

"I just need the trap to take me to the steamer. I have made arrangements to be met on the other side," she added.

"How long do you intend to stay?"

"I'm not sure. Perhaps for good," she said, with a gesture that waved him out of consideration.

"If that's your wish, then so be it." He left the room quietly without another word.

The news of Julia's departure was received with delight by all but Cassie. Her fears for their future at the rectory loomed up again. Without the constant demands of Julia, she would be no longer needed she reasoned. Her memories of less than a year ago were still very real and frightening. These were memories that she could never fully share, memories of fear and suffering that were never very far from the surface. Although she feared and hated Julia Briggs, she gave her a felling of being needed; a reason for being in the house, and that represented a sort of security in her mind.

Marcia on the other hand, knew only too well that she would be back to torment them again. After all, there was a limit to the patience of even her mother's own sister. But a little while of peace was non the less welcome. Ellen's thoughts went back to her conversation with the Reverend and thought with Julia gone, this would be an opportune time to bring the topic up again.
Two days later everything was all to change, when she found Maggie lying unconscious at the bottom of the stairs. She had heard the horrible thud of her fall from where she was working in the kitchen.

Summonsing help, they carried her back upstairs

and laid her in her bed. The doctor came but, he only shook his head; there was nothing he could do. She died shortly afterwards without regaining consciousness.

Ellen and Cassie sat weeping beside her still body for most of the night, for they had grown to love her in spite of her strange wee, ways. The kitchen seemed an empty and forlorn place without her and her chair.

On the night before her funeral, Henry went to his wife's room.

"The funeral is at eleven o'clock. We will leave here at ten thirty, and it's only fitting that we should all be there."

"Why are you telling me?"

"Because it's only fitting that you should be there. She served us faithfully all these years, enduring your wrath again, and again, without complaint."

"I have no intention of going to her funeral Henry. Now will you go?"

Now, all his feelings were suspended by an intense and unfamiliar resentment and in that moment he knew that he hated her.

They followed Maggie's funeral in the trap, and had little to say to each other as they drove along. Their hearts were too full for trivial conversation.

"I can't believe that mother didn't think it worth her while to come with us," Marcia said, as if speaking to herself. The mention of her name sent shivers down

Henry's spine. Glancing at his strained expression made Marcia aware of how deeply sad he really was, and her heart went out to him.

They laid her to rest beside the moss grey stones, where her parents and grandparents lay. And, apart from they themselves there was no one left to mourn her passing.

Following the funeral, they returned to the rectory where Lizzy had made hot soup, which lifted their spirits a little. Ellen, Cassie and Marcia sat in the kitchen in silence, while the silent Lizzie made them tea. The silence was rudely interrupted by the gangling bell from Julia's room. Cassie rose to answer it and Marcia heaved a sigh. When Cassie hadn't returned twenty minutes later, Marcia went to investigate. As she neared her door she could hear her mother's angry voice from within,

"fold them properly you stupid girl. At least I will have a proper ladies maid when I get home, and not a stupid clumsy imbecile like you." Marcia stood listening with mounting rage welling up inside her. Then she reminded herself that she would soon be gone, and that anyway shouting her rage at her would be useless. And so she went inside to rescue wee Cassie and remained silent, while inside her emotions crossed between despair and rage.

A few days later the Reverend appeared in the kitchen, and seated himself at the big wooden table.

"I need to talk to you both," he said, getting up and pulling out two chairs opposite indicating, for them to sit down. When they were seated he began again, "now that Maggie is no longer with us, we need to talk about the future. Ellen would you be willing to take over her job? The pay isn't very big. But, it would give you a bit of financial independence." Ellen remained silent for the few seconds pause that followed, while Cassie cried out inwardly, 'please say you will. Please.' "Now, I don't want you to agree out of any sense of duty. You owe me nothing. And if you need time to think about it, then that's fine too."

At last, Ellen spoke much to Cassie's relief.

"I'm not nearly as good a cook as Maggie was. But, I'll give it a go."

Cassie's relief, at her mother's answer was quickly replaced by fear at his next words.

"I haven't forgotten about that conversation we had about your own place. In fact, I have arranged for the roof of a wee cottage near here to be thatched. The family that lived there went to America. Anyhow, if you want to live away from the house here, it's there for you." Jumping to her feet, Cassie's voice rang out in near hysteria,

"no—no---I won't go to any wee cottage. Please," she ended, sobbing out of control.

"Cassie. What is it? You are welcome to stay here forever, for my part. All I was saying, was that the cottage is there if you should want it."

"Sorry Reverend. I didn't tell her about wanting a place of my own."

Glancing at Cassie with a look of pained surprise, she said crossly,

"stop it Cassie. You're shaming me."

"Don't worry about it Ellen. She feels insecure, that's all. And not much wonder after all she's been through. Oh, and about Maggie. She left a sum of money, not a very big sum. But, as she has no relations I'm sure she would like you to have it." He paused for a second, then added, after all she couldn't have managed these past twelve months without your help."

Then from his pocket he took out a small cloth pouch, and handed it to Ellen.

"I don't know what to say."

"Just take it. You've earned it."

With that he got up from the table, and went over to where Cassie sat. Reaching down, he touched her cheek gently, before saying,

"try to be happy Cassie. And I promise that while I live, you will never, be evicted again. The famine has been devastating to our people. But, bad as it is here, other parts suffered far worse. It is said that the population will be halved, what with death and emigration. We can only pray for a disease free potato crop this year." With that he left the kitchen. When he closed the door behind him, Ellen said angrily.

"Why did you shame me like that? And, the poor man doing all he could to get me a wee place of my own, like I asked him."

"I don't want to go to any wee place. I want to stay here. I won't go," she added with tears again filling her eyes. Looking at her fearful appearance, the mock show of defiance in her voice didn't fool Ellen. Going over to where she sat, Ellen picked her up from the chair,

"poor wee Cassie. My poor wee Cassie, you've had a hard time of it," she said, rocking her back and forth in her arms. Will you at least look at the wee place that's being re-thatched, and if you don't like it then we'll stay put."

"I won't like it," her muffled voice came back.

"Well like I said. If you don't like it then we'll stay put. Oh! I forgot about Ellen's money. Will we count it?" Jumping down out of her arms Cassie grinned broadly through her tears,

"I wonder how much is in it?"

"Well, whatever's in it will be twice as much as we have now."

When they at last finished counting, they were over seventeen pounds better off.

"God bless you Ellen. I will always remember you in my prayers, for as long as I live. It's long and many a day, since I had anything to call my own," she added with a hint of a smile.

John Brown's remains were buried on the same day as Maggie, following a quiet service in the local church. Reverend Bedford agreed to see to the arrangements and the burial, much to Henry's relief. The news of his murder was still rife in the parish for weeks following the funeral. As he went about his duties, he saw groups of people on corners and at crossroads deep in conversation, and he could sense relief in their faces. Rumour was rife in the neighbourhood about his replacement. It was said that he was sent down from Dublin, and was only rarely seen outside the gate lodge where he was living. The police investigation had revealed nothing; no one saw anything out the ordinary it seemed, and it was everyone's wish that they never would. The big house remained empty despite rumours that his lordship's son was about to return. The gardeners still toiled around the house and in the big walled garden, and Mary McDermott, remained as housekeeper. She dusted and aired the big lofty, empty rooms lighting a fire in a different room each day. With John Brown no longer around shouting his orders, she was free to do as she wished.

Soon the murder ceased to be news, and for the time being at least, the evictions stopped. But, still the emigration of the young continued like a haemorrhage, leaving sadness in its wake. Those who found work sent whatever few dollars they could spare home to parents, thus easing their hardships a little.

Henry Briggs drove the pony and trap along the long
stretch of narrow, rocky road that ran along the coast.
His wife sat silently adjacent surrounded by her
numerous pieces of luggage. They had nothing of any
consequence to say to each other, and yet for his part
Henry felt that there were too many things left unsaid.
He regarded her uneasily, her expression was ominous,
her brows knit into a scowl.

He reminded himself that they had loved each other
once, although he found that nearly impossible to believe
at this moment. It pained him to remember how cold and
unfeeling the farewell between mother and daughter had
been earlier. Marcia had dutiful kissed her lightly on the
cheek, and Julia showed no signs of affection or emotion,
when she turned and boarded the trap without glancing
back at her only daughter. It had been a cold and
unfeeling affair, which left him with a deep sense of
sadness. As they neared the dock, he asked quietly,

"is there anything else you would like me to do for
you in your absence?"

"Nothing. I will be back for Harry when he finishes
that damned school that you sent him to. And, I will
expect him to spend the summers with his aunt and me in
the meantime. That's my only regret. If I hadn't been ill,
you wouldn't have had the chance to take him away from
his excellent boarding school."

"Come off it, Julia. The poor wee lad was nearly dead. And it was that, 'excellent school' as you put it that wrote to tell me how ill the poor wee fellow was."

She looked at him with hatred in her eyes, and the muscles around her tight set mouth twitched,

"You will never gain control of my son. Never.... I will kill you first." The look of hate and the menace in her voice made him recoil from any further attempt to reason with her. Could she be insane he wondered? Right now it seemed to be the only explanation that he could allow himself to contemplate. His thoughts went back to his own mother, and how the happiness and wellbeing of her children were her only concern. And, he wondered again at how he didn't rely on this background when choosing his partner. Then, with a start, he wondered if these cold and unfeeling traits could be passed on to their children. He thought first of Marcia; kind caring Marcia who gave her all for those less fortunate than herself. Then he thought of sensitive, wee Harry, and how tears would spring into his eyes at the sight of a fellow human in distress, and of how he nursed that wounded cat that he found in the lane. And he thanked God, for the gift of his children.

When he had helped her load her luggage onto the boat, she held out a gloved hand. He shook it lightly, and she was gone.

Ellen found the job of cook a little easier than expected.

With the Madam gone, she had no complaints about her offerings, and she found that Maggie's tuition had paid off. Lizzy came silently every morning to clean and do the laundry, leaving again about two in the afternoon. Ellen noticed a change in Lizzy of late. She had become thin and drawn; a sadder look about her somehow, and she wished that she could communicate with her to find out what was wrong. She noticed that when facing each other, she could lip read a little, and would nod vigorously when she understood.

She was still pondering this dilemma on her way to visit the cottage, as she usually did late in the evening. As she neared it she noticed that the thatching had been completed. She loved it's outlook towards the sea, the sprawling byre and hen house that flanked it; loved the small windows lit red from the setting sun, and the pink rose bush that sprawled around the doorway. She thought of how it must have been when the young family lived there, when it would have echoed with laughter, a babble of voices, the shouts of children, the sound of hurrying feet and of music.

As she stood there in the silence, she wanted more than anything to live there, for this to be her own wee place to belong to. She sighed deeply where she stood, because she knew that to live here now would be almost impossible. Cassie cringed in fear every time she mentioned it. And, then there was her job as cook at the rectory, where she earned their living. She could only hope to spend one day, off a fortnight here and Sunday afternoon. And it would eventually become damp and cold, and where would she get turf for the fire?

These thoughts turned around in her head as she walked slowly back along the rutted laneway.

Cassie sat close to the window writing in her diary as she done every evening, the red glow from the lowering sun lighting up auburn red tinges in her hair. Lifting, her head, from her work, she gazed thoughtfully out the window. As she watched her, Ellen remarked to herself, how much she had grown in the year and a half since they came here. She was scarcely recognisable as the skinny bedraggled wee being that she had been back then. She was growing into a beauty, and those amazing green eyes, that were exact replicas of her father's, reminded her of him every time she looked at her. As she began writing again, a sudden thought dawned on Ellen. She could use paper and a pencil to help her with her communication problem with Lizzy.

The pencil and paper proved to be just the added tool that helped to unlock the silent world that Lizzy inhabited. Although she couldn't write, she was non the less, able to create little drawings and symbols that spoke their own language.

Ellen discovered that Lizzy lived with her brother and sister-in-law, and five of their children in a small cramped house. It seemed that her brother's wife didn't want her there, and let her know that she was in her way. Things had become unbearable since the arrival of the latest baby. Ellen's heart went out to her, and she pondered endlessly on how she could help this gentle soul, who inhabited a lonely, silent world of which there was no escape.

Unable to sleep one night, a possible answer to Lizzy's problem came to her. If the Reverend agreed, Lizzy could move into the newly thatched cottage, and she herself could spend her nights there, her days off and Sunday afternoons. They could keep poultry and grow potatoes in the garden. The idea excited her so much that it rendered her sleepless into the wee hours.

As soon as breakfast was over she knocked on the study door,

"come in," his voice answered. "Sit down Ellen. Is everything all right?"

"Oh, aye. But, I have something I need to ask you. It's about Lizzy----and me, and the cottage." Licking her lips nervously, she went on, "I've learned to communicate with Lizzy through signs and wee drawings on paper, and that. Well she's not wanted at home, and she's very unhappy. Well, I thought that if you agree her and me could move to the cottage. I'd just sleep there at night mind you----my day off and a Sunday afternoon and that. But, Lizzy would have a home where she'd be wanted." She observed his reaction closely, her heart pounding in her ears. Then clearing his throat, he smiled before answering,

"that sounds like a very good idea. And you did well to learn how to make contact with Lizzy.

What does wee, Cassie think?

"Well, I don't know. I didn't tell her yet. I know she won't want to go. But, if I explain she might-------come round to the idea."

"She could always sleep here for now."

"Thanks Reverend. You and Marcia have been that good to us---I'll never be able to repay you."

"You've been good to us too. Think nothing of it," he added, with a dismissive wave of his hand.

On her way back to the kitchen she felt elated that her plan had been agreed to, and yet she hadn't asked Lizzy. 'What if she doesn't want to go at all,' she thought, suddenly deflated.

It took only a short while to communicate her plan to Lizzy. Her face lit up in a broad smile, and she nodded her pleasure and enthusiasm.

That same evening they walked the short distance to the cottage. Turning to Ellen, with joy written on her face, Lizzy clasped her hands together with delight when she saw it. They spent an hour just sitting in the empty cottage and wandering around the deserted garden making silent plans for the future. Ellen thought it amazing that she could feel happy again after all the sorrow that had gone before, and she marvelled at the power and courage of the human spirit to withstand all in its path.

Walking back slowly in the evening light, the cuckoo's cheerful sound echoing, in the still air Ellen gave thanks for the gift of sound and wished that Lizzy too, could hear the hopeful sounds of spring.

Seated by the range fire that evening, she told Cassie about their plans. She watched her face crumple, and tears well in her eyes, before crying out defiantly,

"I won't go with you. I won't. I told you before, I'm staying here."

"All right. I won't force you now. But, I want you with me Cassie."

"I'm not going," she added resistantly, running out of the kitchen to find Marcia.

Marcia was alone in the sitting room, with only the light of the fading embers of the fire for company. Her days seemed to drift by; quiet monotonous days, filled with working and waiting, and the sudden surge of unexpressed resentment and the flat calm of resignation.

Earlier she had taken the pony for a canter on the hills, but neither the pony nor she had much heart. Up on the hills a light wind wrinkled the puddles and stirred the heather. A gleam of sunlight picked up a clump of yellow gorse, and she thought with a stab of the anguish of Johnny far away in his lonely exile. 'Oh, Johnny,

Johnny, I need you now! Why are you so far away, darling Johnny, when I need you so much?' She had a childish feeling that if she thought about Johnny hard enough, longed for him hard enough, she might see him coming over the heather track, his eyes crinkling and his white sound teeth flashing in the kind smile she knew so well. "Hello, brown eyes," he would say, and kiss the top of her nose. But no Johnny came. There was just the bare hills and the whispering heather and the emptiness and her. She turned the pony around and rode back, with tears of self pity stinging her eyes.

When Cassie burst through the door, for once she was in no mood to listen to her troubles. When she trotted out her woes and Marcia for the very first time, seemed preoccupied, and failed to respond, she walked away feeling desolate and alone in her troubles.

When her heart lightened a little, Marcia began to feel guilty about ignoring Cassie's laments, and went in search of her. She was lying alone in the darkness in the room above the kitchen. Lighting the small candle, she went over to where she lay.

"I'm sorry Cassie. I should have listened to your troubles. But, I was in low spirits myself tonight. I'm missing Johnny, and it all seems... so hopeless somehow," she ended in a sigh. Anyway, tell me again about the cottage," she said, trying to sound more cheerful.

"Could I stay here with you?"

"I would like nothing better Cassie. But, what would your mother say about that?"

"She said I could stay here for now."

"Right then, that's settled."

Sitting up in the bed she looked at Marcia thoughtfully in the flickering candle light, and suddenly remembering their seventeen pound inheritance, she asked,

"how much would it cost to go to Canada?"

"I don't rightly know. Why?"

"Because if you had money, and Johnny couldn't come home here, you could go to Canada to see him."

In the silence that followed Marcia contemplated the idea. Why had she never thought of that before? But right on the heels of hope came thoughts of her father.

And then there was Cassie who was also dependent on her. But still, it was a hopeful possibility that lifted her spirits.

Cassie blew out the candle and prayed in darkness that her share of Maggie's legacy would be enough to take Marcia to New Brunswick. Then with a start she thought about what this would mean to her. And so she cancelled the previous prayer, this time asking God to bring Johnny home to her. With that she slept.

Cassie and Ellen had toiled for days weeding the potatoes in the garden at the front of the house. Straightening their aching backs, they saw Marcia walk towards the house with a deep frown on her face. Something is wrong, Cassie thought miserably. She has been avoiding me and locking herself away in the study alone.

From the moment she got the brown paper parcel from Canada, Marcia had become almost like a different person. Cassie was fearful of the future again as she tried to find an explanation that would explain her friend and protector's sudden, strange behaviour.

As she watched the troubled expression on her daughter's face Ellen couldn't help feeling uneasy. Her encounter with Marcia the evening before was still tumbling around in her brain, and would not rest. She had been surprised to find Marcia waiting for her at the cottage, and the reason for her visit had shocked and wounded Ellen deeply. As soon as they were seated Marcia said,

"I'll get right to the point. I've decided to go out to New Brunswick to Johnny for a few years. And, I'd like to take Cassie with me... if you'd agree, that is." Ellen stared at her for a few seconds in disbelief at her words.

Then a deep anger welled up inside her. Jumping to her feet she shouted,

"No. No. She's my waine. She stays here with me. Don't you think I've lost enough already, my husband two of my babies and then my home. Now you have the nerve to ask me to give you the only flesh and blood I've left. Go to New Brunswick. Go on. But you go on your own." Ellen could feel her whole body shake as she lowered herself back into the chair.

Marcia stared at her in silence, her limbs shook and her lips trembled, so shocked was she at the rage she had aroused in Ellen.

"I'm...sorry. I didn't mean to... I wasn't thinking. It's just that I'm so attached to Cassie, and couldn't bear the thought of leaving her behind. "

"To make yourself feel better about letting her down, you decided to just take her with you. Me. I'm only her mother."

"Ellen I'm sorry. Please don't tell Cassie about this. It was a crazy idea anyway."

Getting up she went to the door. Then turning around to Ellen again, she said, "my only excuse is that I care about her. And I suppose I couldn't bear to leave her behind. I promised her I'd always be here for her, you see."

"Where did I fit in eh,? You go to New Brunswick, an' leave us in peace. I may be poor, but not so poor, that I'd give up my own daughter." For an instant Marcia was speechless. Then, making an effort to pull her scattered wits together, she answered;

"I'm sorry. I only meant it to be for a couple of years at the most. "I'm sorry..." she repeated.

A while later Ellen heard her click the latch as she went out the door. She sat there in the silence listening to the quickened, rhythm of her own heart, until her anger subsided. The justifiable anger that she had felt earlier soon gave way to regret. After all Marcia Briggs had been their salvation when they were destitute. And that she had Cassie's best interests at heart, she was in no doubt; and that she would jump at the chance to go with her, she had no doubts about that either. She had to confess to herself that Cassie was far closer to Marcia than she was herself. And, she was jealous of that fact.

Then searching her own conscience, she had to admit that she was mostly to blame. She had been so lost in her own grief she had ignored her child. The loss of Michael and then her home, had drained her of all emotion, leaving only feelings of wasted years devoid of aim and interest. Lost in her own pain, she had shut Cassie out. She knew that Marcia's going would hurt and wound her deeply, and so she made herself a promise that she would do all in her power to make the empty years up to her.

Later that evening a still troubled Cassie, found Marcia alone in the study. She hardly seemed to notice that she was not alone so preoccupied was she in her own thoughts. Cassie cleared her throat and coughed for a full minute or so, before she caught her attention.

"Oh, it's you Cassie. I didn't know you were here. I'm day dreaming you see."

Then she glanced out the window reflectively, and gave a long deep sigh before, she said, as if talking to herself.   "my poor Johnny. What a lot you have seen and endured since you left us."

"Is Johnny sick.?"

"No. No, he's not sick…not now." Then looking back at Cassie's troubled face she smiled, before saying, "Sorry if I've ignored you a lot lately…it's just that I'm trying to make an important decision. And, when I've made it you'll be the first to know."

"Is it to do with the papers you got from Canada?" Marcia nodded.

"Don't look so downhearted Cassie. Tell you what.

We'll go down to the shore before dark, and go to see Johnny's Mammy and Daddy. I gave them the papers that Johnny sent me to read. If they have finished reading it, I'd like you to read it too. You see, he kept a written account of everything that happened since he left…or since he was forced out of here."

They walked to the shore in silence, each lost in their separate thoughts. Johnny's mother greeted them at the door and Marcia noticed that she seemed to be more elated than usual. The talk was all about Johnny.

"Have you finished reading it?" Marcia asked, "I want Cassie to read it too," she explained.

"Aye, I've read it all twice and it's amazing what he's endured, and how far he's come."

"Will you whist woman and let the wee girl read the story for herself," Johnny's father's voice came from the corner in the shadows.   Ignoring her husband's advice, she went on.   "But, he has weathered it all well. And he's learned about life.   He had it easier than most, had Johnny.   Never knew the hunger like so many in this famine.   We always had enough," she added.

Cassie contemplated her for a few seconds before asking,
    "is he all right?
I don't want to know what's in it.   I just want to know if he's all right."

    "Aye, he's all right…now.   That's all I'm saying." Cassie wanted more than ever to know what Johnny's writings were about, for she had a dark feeling that it bore bad tidings for her and that it would explain Marcia's strange behaviour.   But she knew that it would be useless to ask him any more questions.

When they left it was almost dusk.   Nearing the crossroads, they stopped to listen to the sounds of a fiddle echoing on the gentle breeze.   As they came closer, they could see a group of people standing around clapping to the music.   Then a few began to dance in the laneway, swinging in lively rhythm to the quickening tempo of the music.   They seated themselves on the ditch, and watched the scene, tapping their feet in time to the music.   A young fellow from the group spotted them.   Coming over to where they sat, he reached out grabbing Marcia by the hand,

    "come on an' dance."   Before she knew what was

happening she was being swung around, the small stones from the rough surface of the laneway flying through the air. At last exhausted she flung herself down again beside Cassie,

"that was great fun. You try next time," she urged Cassie. And so they danced until darkness was all around them.

"We'll be back same night next week. Will you come?" The young black haired fellow called after them.

"Aye, we'll try. We'll do our best."

When they reached the house all was in darkness. Lighting a candle for Cassie, she walked ahead of her up the stairs. As they reached the door, Cassie said softly,

"to night was good fun. I want to learn to dance better, so I can show Harry how to do it." Then looking at the brown paper parcel in Marcia's hand, she asked, "can I read it now? I want to know all about Johnny... and Canada."

"The morrow?"

"Aye, the morrow," she answered, with a hint of a smile.

"I can have no secrets from you, you wee witch." "Now off you go to bed and don't wake your mother," Marcia whispered as she went.

Lying in the darkness, Cassie thought again about Johnny and the written account he had kept about his journey and his life far away from them. She had never seen him, yet she could picture him clearly in her head. Through Marcia she knew him, and she felt that his life was intertwined with hers. And now more than anything else she wanted to read every word he had written, then she felt she would know what was in Marcia's mind. But the feeling of foreboding persisted leaving her sleepless.

Getting out of bed she went downstairs. Lighting another candle she made her way to the drawing room. She poked the fire back to life and put on a few, turf before lighting the oil lamp. Then she opened the brown paper parcel. And, there she remained until dawn, on a journey that would take her across the Atlantic with Johnny and she would know how his trials and triumphs would affect her life. It was a story that she was to record in her diary with great accuracy.

Chapter 14

The Exiles Journey

Bound by hands and feet, Johnny Maloney sat helplessly in the small rowing boat as it made it's way out to the mouth of the harbour. His thoughts were muddled and his head throbbed as he struggled to free himself. He desperately tried to remember what happened. He knew that he'd been attacked and beaten around the head in the town. But struggle as he might nothing else would come to him.

"Take me back to the shore. You've the wrong man. I'm Johnny Maloney. I'm a boat builder. Where in the hell do you think you're taking me?"

"Just following orders. You're getting a free trip to Canada boyo."

"You've the wrong man. I've done nothing wrong."

"You should have kept clear of the clergyman's daughter," the other rower shouted with a broad leering grin, showing his yellow teeth. Slowly, through the haze of his muddled thoughts, Johnny knew what was happening. It wasn't a mistake; he was being deported out of Marcia's reach. The blood rushed to his face as he struggled again violently to free himself from the ropes.

"Take it easy boyo. Them ropes are tough. And if you had any big ideas about jumping ship, put them right out of your head. You wouldn't last two minutes in these waters."

He was hauled on board the ship; his rib cage bruised and hurting from the rough ropes that bound him. Lying on the deck he watched one of the boatmen hand money to the captain. He counted it out, then nodded. "I'll see that he gets to Saint John in one piece," he said with a wink. From his position lying on the deck he could smell whiskey from his breath. "Get him down below," he ordered the crew, and sauntered off.

His hands and feet still tied together; he lay motionless on the uneven boards of the main cabin. As he gazed into the chilly shadows, he made out forms of the other passengers as they lay huddled in bunks or crouched on the floor. Babies cried out and a chorus of coughs and loud moans filtered into his consciousness. From the gloom a mans voice asked,

"what happened to you? Why you tied up?"

"Untie these ropes. Please," he added, with a grimace, as pain shot through him.

"What did ye' do?" he persisted

"I done nothing. Don't even know why I'm here."

Getting down on his hands and knees the stranger painstakingly untied the tight ropes that bound him.

"Thanks," he said between gritted teeth. The man went back into the shadows, returning with a tin cup of water. He reached for it and drank thirstily. Draped over his shoulder was a thin grey blanket, pulling it down he handed it to him, "no spare blankets or bunks; I brought me own." Johnny thanked him, as he pulled it around his aching body.

And now, began for Johnny a period of intense suffering. Dependent on a casual piece of bread and drink of water, there were days when he ate nothing at all. For brief intervals his memory would fail him, he would lye in a feverish stupor. Sometimes he forgot who he was or where he was. Then the lurching of the boat would remind him that he was at sea.

He wasn't sure how long this state of fever and pain lasted. He was only aware of feeling a little stronger as the days passed. As the sea grew rougher the plight of his fellow passengers penetrated his consciousness, more and more.

The air was foul and reeking with the stench of vomit. The sounds of vomiting and the smells disturbed him to the point where he found the cold wave washed decks more comfortable. With only the thin blanket for warmth, he decided to spend the night huddling under a lifeboat for shelter.

Wrapping the blanket around him, he sank down in the chilly shadows with his hands in his pockets and his back against the wet boards. It was bitterly cold. Johnny drowsed in fitful snatches. Dawn came in a grey and sullen haze. So cold and cramped he could scarcely rise, he became aware of another presence.

"You look frozen to the bone lad," a deep male voice said. "Better come into my cabin for a while."

Inside the small cramped cabin at the side of the deck Johnny sat down on a trunk. "Better get into my bunk for a while 'till you thaw out a bit. It'll still be warm, for I just got out of it. What took you out on the deck to sleep?" he asked when Johnny had snuggled down.

"Conditions below are awful. Overcrowded and everybody sick...and the smell."

"Must be bad when you preferred to nigh on freeze to death."

"Aye it's that bad."

"My name's Joseph Conrad by the way"

"Mine's Johnny Maloney," he said holding out a trembling hand from beneath the blanket.

"Aren't you the young fellow that was hauled on board just before we sailed?" the man asked, shaking his hand, and peered closely at him.

"Aye, that was me."

Looking at Johnny again, he asked,

"if it's not an impertinent question, why were you

tied up?

"I'm not a murderer or anything, if that's what you're thinking."

Then with a dismissive gesture, he said,

"it's none of my business. Forget I asked."

Ignoring his gesture Johnny went on,

"the truth is I'm not right sure myself. But I have strong suspicions. I was set about in the town. Hit over the head with something. Then the next thing I remember was being in a wee boat and being thrown on here. Bound for Saint John, New Brunswick I'm told."

During the hour or so that followed Johnny told the stranger about his love for Marcia Briggs, and how he suspected her mother and John Brown were responsible for his present plight.

"But, I won't know for sure 'till I hear from home. All I have is the tattered rags I stand up in," he ended.

Joseph Conrad studied him closely for a minute or so, before he spoke,

"that's about the sorriest tale I heard in a long while. And God, only knows you only have to look at the miserable wretches below to see sorrow. But, Johnny, you are young and strong and you'll survive. You'll get work in Saint John. I've heard it's a promising place. And, when you've made enough go back and claim that girl. Show them. Aye, show them that they can't keep a good man down." Johnny grinned, his white teeth gleaming through the gloom of the cabin.

"Thanks. You've made me feel better,"

"Good. But one more thing, if you want to stay alive don't spend another night out there. You can sleep here on the floor if you want. Not much space, but better than freezing to death eh?"

"I'm in your debt."

"Think nothing of it. I happened to have a few more shillings than you do; otherwise I too would be below. This rat infested crate is not fit to carry passengers. It's nothing short of a crime to pack all them poor souls into a ship like this. It's only fit for cargo."

"Is there no laws about the kind of ships, that's used for this number of passengers?" Johnny asked.

"Aye, there's laws, but the law is not enforced. Greed...greedy ship owners taking advantage of desperate people."

Then going over to the trunk, he rummaged around for a while, and returned with a pair of trousers and a sweater.

"These will do you a turn. And this will keep you from going insane." He gave him a few folded sheets of writing paper and a pencil. "Write it all down son, starting today, the thirty first of April eighteen fifty. Maybe you can make somebody listen; somebody will want to know about these horrors some day."

"I don't know what I'd a done if I hadn't fallen in with you," Johnny said, with gratitude in his voice.

"You'd have managed. Aye you'd have managed."

In the days that followed Joseph shared his meagre rations with Johnny, "wouldn't eat it all myself anyway," he'd argue. But Johnny knew he was lying. As his strength grew he went below to offer what help he could to the other passengers. Some of them grew sicker as the voyage grew longer. He watched a young woman not much older than he was himself, die in an overcrowded bunk with filthy grey blankets. The sick woman had lain in her bunk like a corpse in its coffin. The oil lamp swinging from one of the low transverse beams, threw out a pale sickly light, making pearls of the beads of perspiration that clung to her face and matted her hair into a dank dark tangle. The plank sided bunks and narrow deal table bolted to the floor took up all available space; it was as dark and cheerless as a dungeon. Johnny silently vowed to the dying woman, in that bleak moment, that he would somehow try to bring the horrors of her suffering and that of his fellow passengers to the notice of the powers that be. When she finally died he could only feel an immense relief.

Following a few prayers on deck, her body was unceremoniously dumped overboard. Two days later, her baby went much the same way. He had listened to the cries become weaker, and he had gone out on deck, pounding his fists against the rough timbers in a helpless gesture against the suffering of his fellow human beings.

Then the crying stopped, and all his nerves strained out onto the silence, and he wept.

And each day he put down his thoughts on paper. The relief of this act kept his spirits just high enough to face another day.

When he slept his dreams were of Marcia; he could see her soft brown eyes, smell her scent, and stroke her soft hair. Then he would awake with a start, and the pain of missing her would begin all over again. He felt close to her when he wrote down his thoughts, hoping that she would one day read them. But this would only happen when he had something to offer her. He would think longingly of his parents and the cottage at home, tucked tightly into it's own little headland and he would sigh deeply with longing.

As the days passed the food rations got even smaller. Hungry drawn faces with a look of desperation in their eyes as they scanned the seas for sight of land. At last on a grey dawn Johnny heard a seagull overhead. Then he spotted the first sight of land. He closed his eyes for a few seconds, then opened them again to be sure that it was indeed the land that he saw. Then filling his lungs he shouted, "Land. Land ahead." Within minutes the deck was crowded with passengers. They stood in silence shivering, as they held their thin grey blankets around their skinny bodies for protection against the chilly dawn.

Tears of relief filled their eyes as they stood silently

watching the land showing in the distance. There was no sound but the sighing wind and the murmur of the waves breaking against the boat as they gave silent thanks to the Almighty for their deliverance.

Joseph's voice broke the poignant silence, "may it truly be the land of promise, for, God knows we deserve it." Murmurs of 'Amen' echoed among them.

As the sun rose high the decks became a hive of activity. Sea water was hauled aboard to wash away the dirt and smells of their body's and of their clothing, and they dressed in whatever half- decent clothing they owned.

When at last they reached the dock they had to remain on board until they had been inspected for contagious diseases. Coming up beside Johnny, Joseph remarked,

"the final indignity." Then he handed him a small parcel wrapped in a piece of brown cloth; "it's not much. But it will tide you over. Always stand up for your rights, and get back and marry that girl of yours when you're able." Then reaching out his hand, he said solemnly, "I hope we'll meet again."

Johnny shook the hand that was held out firmly,

"I hope we meet again too. I will never forget you, for you restored my faith in humankind."

At the foot of the gangplank he gave Joseph a final salute as he disappeared into the crowd.

Chapter 15

The New World

By the late afternoon Johnny finally found a room that was habitable. The boarding houses he had looked at near the docks were overcrowded, some of them filthy. Then he spotted the small sign in the window of a house that said 'room to let.' The room was small, and in the attic, but it was clean. A young family from County Antrim occupied the other three rooms on the middle floor. They had four small children and another one soon to be born. Martha was a friendly young woman who looked far older than her twenty-five years. She and her husband James had been in Saint John for almost two years and she painted a grim enough picture of life there.

"It's tough going for the Irish here now. So many have come looking for work since the famine, and there is prejudice against us," she told Johnny. "The voyage across the ocean was something I'll never forget. The conditions were awful...awful. But, we were lucky that the fever didn't break out among us. The poor creaters that had to be quarantined on the island. It was awful,

awful. Read about it in the newspapers. Trying to escape the hunger at home, an' all they found here was a grave.

But there is still work to be had. It has to be better than what we left behind." Then she gazed into the distance with a wishful expression, "I miss home sometimes. I miss my mother and father. I miss the green hills and valleys, an' the story telling on winter nights an' the music. But I will never see it again. Aye, in spite of everything it'll always be home." Then looking down at her children where they played on the floor, she said, "when I tell them about it, they won't even know what I'm talking about."

They were interrupted by the sound of heavy footsteps on the hollow wooden stairs. "That'll be James; my husband," she said, getting to her feet, "better get his supper, he'll be starving." That's one consolation here, there's enough to eat. Mind you I've seen many of the immigrants begging in the streets; so we're fortunate." James was a burley, powerful, man of six foot with a surly disposition to match. He greeted Johnny with only a grunt of acknowledgement. Later when they had eaten supper he ventured to ask him about where he would find work. "The docks is about the only place around here. They pay a dollar a day. And by God ye' work for it."
Johnny wanted to find out more, but he bid him a surly goodnight, and went to bed.

The following morning Johnny stood in line at the

docks waiting to be hired. At last his turn came to be scrutinised by the foreman for size and strength. He looked at him for a few seconds in silence, before saying,

"I'll give you a try. But if you don't shape up then, you're out. Next," he yelled.

And so began Johnny's first day of back breaking work as a dock labourer.

For weeks he would return to the lodging house so weary and muscle sore, that he had just enough energy left to eat and fall into his attic bed. On Sundays, he wrote letters home, and filled in what little there was to say about his over worked days in the docks in his record of events, that he had promised Joseph he would keep.

He walked into the post office, as he had done twice weekly, for the past six weeks, hoping for a letter from home.

"Johnny Maloney," he said, when his turn came.

"You're in luck the day. There's two for you," he said, turning to the boxes on the wall behind him.

"Thanks, thanks," he said half running outside, so great was his relief.

He found a quiet place along the quayside, and sat down to read the letters from his mother and Marcia. Before opening Marcia's letter, he sat holding it reverently between his fingers. It was the first time he had ever seen her handwriting, and it was happiness enough just to look at it. He read both letters again and again before getting to his feet. As he walked back to his attic, his steps felt lighter and there was a song in his heart again. Neither the noise of the baby's, almost constant cries, nor, the quarrelling from the street below could annoy him tonight. Taking out the letters from his pocket he read them again before falling asleep.

Chapter 16

The Hand Of Fate

Johnny awoke from a restless sleep, and rubbed the sweat from his eyes. He hated this hot and sultry July weather, that was rendering his usual Sunday afternoon sleep impossible. In the room below him, the baby cried and the older children quarrelled incessantly. His mind was befuddled with the din and with the oppressive heat and his head throbbed in protest. In these moments of private bitterness, he hated the cruel, evil, injustice that brought him to this juncture. 'Damned cruel, evil bastards,' he repeated over and over again, thumping the grey sweaty pillows. Getting out of bed, he hastily dressed and went outside into the unusually quiet street. He walked away from the grimy streets and towards the sea. Soon he was in a smart, affluent neighbourhood with long, curving driveways leading to big houses shaded by tall, leafy trees. He headed away from the houses and on to the foreshore where, he stripped off and dived into the water. He had always been a strong swimmer, and he swam a good distance out, before turning back again towards the shore. Half an hour later he was lying on the foreshore dozing, to the sound of the lapping water, when he was aroused by the sound of a woman's screams for help. Lifting himself up on his elbow he looked around him for a while. Then he saw her standing alone in the water, as she screamed,

"help... help... he's drowning. Somebody, help." Jumping up, he ran towards her. "It's my brother. He's drowning. Out there," she screamed hysterically and pointed out in front of her. Johnny ran out into the water in the direction she had indicated. Then he saw a head bob up for a second in front of him. He swam out towards it, desperately trying to locate him again.

Then his arm knocked against something solid close to the surface of the water. He grabbed at it, and with relief discovered that it was the drowning man. With a struggle he managed to get his head out of the water. And swam with the limp figure towards the shore. The woman came to help him drag the lifeless form out of the water. He lay on the sand, white and motionless. "My God he's dead...he's drowned," the young woman screamed repeatedly. Bending down Johnny lifted his arm and on laying a finger on his wrist, could just feel the blood pulsating faintly. He quickly turned him over and thumped his back repeatedly, and then he heard a faint splutter as water began spurting from his mouth. He gasped repeatedly for a minute or so, before his breathing became regular. Looking up at the young woman, he smiled, "he'll be ok."

"Thank you. From the bottom of my heart I thank you," she said tearfully. Then getting down on her hands and knees she bent over the man on the ground," Oh, Peter, Peter... I thought you were gone. Are you all right?"

He nodded, indicating that he was. When they helped him to his feet, he staggered backwards,

"I want to sit down for a while," he said in a hoarse whisper.

A few minutes later they helped him to his feet again and he took a few staggery steps forward, while his face remained ashen. Until today, Peter Morris had been blessed, like everyone else, with a fine ability to think only shallowly and seldom of his own end. But just, how close he had come to death shook him to the core.

"Will you help me to get him home?" his sister asked, her mouth trembling, as she spoke. "It's not far away. I'm Jane Morris by the way. I'm still shaking all over. It's only now, what nearly happened is coming home to me. If you hadn't been there... he'd be gone;" she went on, as they struggled along the driveway leading to a big elegant looking house surrounded by tall trees.

They helped Peter up the wide steps. Jane pulled the bell rope and waited. A small grey haired woman in a white apron opened the door. She stood open mouthed regarding them for a few seconds, before asking,

"what happened?"

"Tell mother we want her downstairs. Peter went out of his depth in the water. But, he's all right," she added hastily.

"God, save us all." Get him inside quick. I'll get your mother," she said, scurrying off inside the house.

As they made their way to a door at the right of the big hall, Peter said,

"I'm all right now. I can manage on my own." He stumbled forward shakily towards the door, grabbing on to the handle to steady himself. A tall elegantly dressed woman appeared just as they were helping him onto a sofa. She rushed over to where he lay, her skirts rustling.

"What's wrong. What's happened to Peter?" she demanded.

"I went out too far in the water. This fellow saved me." Then looking up at Johnny, he said, "and I don't believe I thanked him properly."

Looking at Johnny for the first time, she said, in a trembling voice,

"thank you. You will never know just how much I'm in your debt."

Then turning back to her son, she suggested he lie down in his room for a rest, "are you sure you're all right?" she asked anxiously, as he got to his feet.

"I'm fine, honestly," he assured her as he went out of the room.

When he had gone Jane gave her the details of events that almost ended in tragedy. When she had finished, her mother covered her face with a handkerchief and sat in silence for a minute or so before she spoke,

"there had to be someone watching over us this day. I just couldn't contemplate...not after your father," she broke off in a long sigh. Then getting to her feet she said, "I'll just go and see how he's doing. Won't be a minute."

Johnny stood up too,

"think, I better go. I left my shirt on the beach," he added, suddenly remembering his bare chest.

She swung around, and in a voice raised in near panic, she said,

"no, please. Please stay...we must talk. Jane will find you a shirt. And I'll only be a minute," she added hastily, her hand raised towards where Johnny stood, "I'll only be a minute," she repeated.

Left alone Johnny looked around the big ornately furnished room, 'so this is how it is when you make it in this brave new world,' he whispered inwardly. It was a world away from the dinghy cramped attic and the grubby docks. He tried to imagine himself and Marcia in such a setting. Jane's returning with a shirt over her arm interrupted his thoughts,

"hope this will do," she said, handing him the shirt.

My mother wants you to stay for dinner, so she can thank you properly." She sat down on a chair opposite him, and watched him closely as he buttoned the shirt. "I can't tell you how brave I think you are," she said gently.

"It's no more than anyone would have done." Putting up her hand to silence him, she went on,

"oh, but it is. If Peter...had drowned," she shuddered, wiping a tear from her cheek roughly before going on, "my father was killed less than six months ago. A horse in the stables here kicked him. And, now to think that Peter was nearly lost to us as well. Thank you seems so...so inadequate," she said, her voice breaking. Johnny looked across at her, and found her looking at him with an expression that was startling. It was a desperate appeal for understanding that unnerved him.

"I'm sorry about your... father," he faltered.

"My mother was just beginning to get over that shock, when this happened; or nearly happened."

"What did your father do? for a living I mean."

"He owned a newspaper. My mother's taken it over. She was going to sell it at first. But now she's running it herself. What do you do for a living?"

"I'm a dock worker."

"What kind of work does a dock worker do?"

"Loading and unloading ships. It's hard back breaking, labour," he added, annoyed by her ignorance.

A noise from the doorway made them turn their heads,

"how is he now Mama?" Jane asked, as her mother sat down.

"I think he'll be fine. A bit tired that's all."

A gong sounded in the distance. "Dinner's ready.

Come Johnny," she said, getting to her feet.

The dining room was spacious and elegant, with a long oak table in the center. At one end three places were set for the meal. When Jane and her mother were seated Johnny sat down a little nervously. A refreshing pine scented breeze drifted in from the sea through the open window, which in the glow of the setting sun flashed with rosy splendour and mingled its low voice with the voices of the two women. Johnny wondered how the day that began so badly, had placed him in such a strange setting.

He was hungry and the meal tasted good.

Mrs. Morris seemed to eat very little of her meal, and moved it around the plate absently. When the meal was over she said,

"Johnny, will you come with me into the drawing room? I'd like to talk to you"

When they were seated, she looked at him with troubled eyes before she said, "I would like to give you some kind of reward for what you did today. Would I insult you, if I offered you money?"

"I didn't do it for money. Anybody would have done the same in my shoes."

Then with a quick pang of regret, he remembered just how much he needed more money. He hated his stupid pride and in that second wished he could take back his words. Then she asked,

"what then, would you like me to do for you? I must do something. You must have some dreams that I might be able to help come true."

"Right now my dreams are small too paltry to be called dreams at all, and yet they keep me interested in living and hoping."

"Want to tell me about them?" she asked. The quiet serene, voice and kindly eyes prompted Johnny to tell her his story.

When he had finished they sat in silence for a while. Then Johnny said,

"your daughter told me that you own a newspaper." She nodded.

"Well," he went on, "I would like you to write a story for me. Tell your readers of the awful conditions on that ship. It might help them that have to cross the Atlantic in future. That's what I'd like you to do for me."

She looked at him in silence for a few seconds before she spoke.

"Johnny I'd love to do just that. In fact as I was listening to you a few minutes ago, I was about to ask you if I could let the people of this city know, what you and the others endured and are still enduring. I asked if I could do something for you, and now it seems that it's the other way 'round."

"I wrote about it myself, on the journey and that. I could lend it to you if you want."

"That would be a good help. You were saying that you were a boat builder."

"Aye, that's right."

"Could you not have got the same job here?"

He shook his head;

"jobs like that are not easy got."

"Leave it with me. My late husband had interests in the shipbuilding business. I sold it. But they still owe me a favour or two. Just leave it with me."

He gave her a broad smile, as hope flooded through him. Then she said, "I'll call to your lodgings tomorrow for your writings, if you give me your address."

"All right. But, it's a rough place," he warned.

"I want to see where you live. I'll be there."

They regarded each other in silence for a while, then she said, "it's been an amazing day and you're an amazing young man. First, you save my son's life. Then you tell me an amazing story of a world I know nothing about." Then she looked out the window towards the rising moon, with a sad, wishful expression, before saying, "my husband's mother was Irish. He was very proud of that fact, and now I know why."

He got up to go.

"Thank you for the dinner," he said. Getting to her feet, she took both his hands in hers, "thank you sounds so insufficient. But I'll see you tomorrow."

"I don't finish at the docks 'till eight."

"Don't go in tomorrow. Trust me," she added, with determination in her tone.

"Right 'ye are. I won't then," he said, pushing back

his hair with a gesture of relief, he stood looking at her as if dropping his cares completely.

"Will you find your way back? You could stay the night you know."

"I'll find it all right. It's a grand night, 'an the walk will do me good."

She walked outside with him, and they lingered for a while in silence. The air was cool and refreshing and they breathed deeply.

"Oh, by the way Peter wanted to see you before you went. But, he's asleep now. We'll just let him sleep for now, and he'll see you tomorrow."

"No need," Johnny interrupted, "he needs to rest. And anyhow, he gave me his thanks already."

When he reached the gateway, he turned and looked back to where she stood, silhouetted in the moonlight. He waved a brief salute, and walked back towards the grim, rundown neighbourhood and his room in the attic. He found the transition back to it's harsh reality difficult.

Before he went to bed he wrote down his account of the days events. As he got the tattered pages in order, he wondered if this woman from that other world, he had glimpsed so briefly would remain true to her word. Somehow, he believed she would.

In the early afternoon, Johnny was sitting on the front steps of the house when he saw a horse drawn van drive up the street, with 'SAINT JOHN POST' written in big bold lettering. A young man in a smart black suit jumped down onto the pavement,

"I'm looking for Johnny Maloney."

"You found him."

"Mrs. Morris asked me to collect your writing. She says she's sorry she couldn't make it herself today. She didn't want to leave her son just yet. But says, to tell you he's doing ok, and she'll come to see you in a day or two."

Johnny handed him the small brown paper parcel that he had ready and waiting by his side.

"And you're to go to this address at ten in the morning," the stranger added, jumping into the van before Johnny had time to ask for directions.

The following morning Johnny walked along a wide, sweeping dockyard until he found 'John Hall and Sons Shipbuilders.' He was directed to an office at the end of a long low building.

He knocked on the first door he came to,

"come in," a male voice echoed from within.

"I'm Johnny Maloney," he said to the man sitting at the big desk. "I'm looking for Mr. John Hall."

"Sit down. I'm John Hall."

The man in the big armchair across the desk looked formidable and expensive. Johnny looked down at his own dusty, wrinkled black trousers and unconsciously gave a hitch to his sagging coat. Then he held out his hand,

"glad to meet you Mr. Hall. Good of you to see me."

"A pleasure," he said, shaking his outstretched hand. "I have a letter here from Mrs. Morris. She's a fine woman. Her late husband was my partner. Anyhow, she says you're a hero of the highest order, and that you need a helping hand by way of a job."

"Aye, that's about the height of it."

"She says you were a boat builder back in Ireland." Johnny nodded,

"just small fishing boats. But I served my time in a fairly big boat yard. I'm a good carpenter."

John Hall gave him a long searching look before he spoke again,

"the ship we're building now, is a cargo vessel. And we're always in need of good carpenters. So, you're hired," he said, reaching his hand across the desk. Johnny took the outstretched hand and shook it firmly.

"I won't let you down."

"Good. Now I'll show you down to the fitting shed, and introduce you to the foreman. The pay is two dollars a day. But, if your work is good, well, then it might be increased."

Johnny's first weeks at the shipyard were difficult ones. That John Hall, in person introduced him to the foreman was a bad beginning for Johnny. The big boss very seldom came anywhere near the workmen, and that he came in person to introduce a new carpenter, smacked of favouritism from their point of view and they showed their scorn for him at every available opportunity. These were hard days for Johnny, and yet he liked the work which to the foreman's great disappointment, he could find no fault with. The increase in wages gave him a chance to save, and this was his main consolation.

He hadn't really expected to see Mrs. Morris again in spit of the message sent via the van boy; after all she had done her duty in getting him the job. So, it was with surprise that he found her waiting for him at the lodging house one evening when he got home from work. She looked out of place in the dreary kitchen, smelling of bacon and stale cabbage, dressed in her expensive taffeta's and feather decked bonnet. When she saw him her face relaxed in a slow smile,

"I've been waiting for you Johnny," she said softly.

I've got something I need your approval for before it goes to print. And I must say your written account of… everything is very good. So, with your approval, I'd like to let other folks read it."

Studying her across the table Johnny thought what a handsome woman she still was, and what a beauty she must have been in her youth and he wondered if Marcia would look like that in later life. Then he said,

"I'm sure you've done a good job. No need to read

it first."

"Very well then it goes to print. But, I must warn you that I've told your whole story, not just about the voyage and saving my son's life." Her eyes were intent and there was an air of excitement about her, as she went on. "I've told about your life in Ireland and your...er, deportation." Her eyebrows arched into a question mark, before she added, "and about Marcia." When he made no reply, she looked somewhat deflated. Then she asked in a quiet voice, "now do you want to read it first?"

"No. I've no need to read it. Just go ahead and print it. That's if you really think that your readers will want to read it. But, like I said before, I want you to let the people of this city know about the awful conditions on that ship."

"Oh, they'll want to read it all right," she added smiling broadly. And I quoted your account of the conditions on the ship almost word for word."

With that she handed him back the bundle of papers containing his writings, "keep writing Johnny. You have a true gift for it, because I was right there with you every step of your journey. And I even shed a tear or two," she added. When she got to the kitchen door she looked back at him and asked, how's the new job?"

"It's grand. Thanks for putting a word in for me. I earn a dollar a day more, and the work's not as hard."

"Good. Good," she repeated and was gone.

Chapter 17

The Shipbuilder

Two weeks later, Johnny was making his way down the steps of the dockside jetty where he usually went for his midday break, when he heard his name called from behind. John Hall stood at the top of the steps, straightening his cravat,

"glad I caught you. Been reading all about you in the Globe. Seems you're a hero," he added, holding an outstretched hand towards Johnny. Johnny looked puzzled for a few seconds.

"Oh, the newspaper. I forgot about it."

"You mean you haven't seen it yet.?" Johnny shook his head, and shugged his shoulders. "Everyone's talking about it. Even in the bank, it was the main topic of conversation, you're famous lad," he bellowed, with a broad smile.

"Come up to the office with me. Something I'd like to talk to you about."

Johnny followed him along the low building and up the steps to a big outer office where two rows of clerks, seated at long counters bent their heads industriously over their ledgers. Once inside his private office, John Hall motioned him to a big chair then sat down opposite him.

His sharp eyes seemed to size Johnny up for a few seconds before he spoke.

"I read that your voyage across the Atlantic was a rough one, and that you're interested in better ships." Johnny nodded. "Well, I've got an interesting proposition to put to you. My nephew has a bee in his bonnet about steam liners. Bigger and better passenger ships. He hawked his designs from shipping company to shipping company only to be met with derision, until he came to me that is. My argument was that, the wind blows free for every man's use, and that steamships were more expensive to build and run and the bigger steam engines take up to much valuable space. But he pointed out the advantages very persuasively.

Like the shortest distance between two points is a straight line. Anyhow, I decided to back his plan."

Johnny sized up his steel grey eyes and sharp earnest face, that confirmed his reputation of being a tough business man, who wouldn't let, family loyalties interfere with a sound business judgement. In the silence that followed, Johnny wondered where this was leading, and why he was singling him out for special attention. If Johnny at that moment could have read his thoughts he would have understood. John Hall was intent on winning the affections of Catherine Morris, his late partner's wife.

He had been completely besotted by her since their

first meeting over twenty years earlier. And, now was his chance to win her, although he knew only too well that he had an uphill struggle, because she was still grieving for the man she loved and lost. Then, when he read the story of Johnny Maloney, that she had written with such depth of feeling he hoped to win her approval by helping him on his way to a better future.

"I hear times are bad in Ireland. And they've been bad this end too. Far too much death from disease on the voyages and death awaiting them on this side as well. A terrible tragedy."

"Aye, It's bad. But, it wasn't the famine that drove me out."

He nodded solemnly, not taking his eyes from his face.

"Getting back to what I was saying about the steamship that's about to be built. You could learn all about building it; be in at the start of a new era. Start by getting to understand the plans. Be my nephews right hand man, so to speak. It would be a golden opportunity for a young man like yourself who's interested in the business of ships." Johnny looked sharply at him, and read an inflexibility of purpose. By God, he thought, he means it. He needed time to think this offer through. The bait of the new venture in shipbuilding so brazenly dangled before him sent waves of excitement running through his veins. It was what he had always wanted to do, as far back as he could remember. Oh, he had built wee fishing boats, but he had always dreamt about big ships. And the mere thought of being part of something new, added even more to his feeling of excitement. And that he could maybe contribute to better conditions for the passengers of the future gave an added sense of purpose. Then right on the heels of elation came thoughts of Marcia and the hope of going back to her that had kept him sane during the long months of hardship and loneliness. Looking back at John Hall he said,

"I'm tempted and honoured by your offer. But, you see I'm intending to go back home. I've been saving every cent I can to get back."

"Would Mars..Marcia, have anything to do with it?"

A look of surprise crossed Johnny's face,

"how did you know?

"The newspaper. Remember?"

"Oh, I forgot about that. Looks like I'm an open book." John Hall gazed into space in silence for a while, before saying quietly as if talking to himself, "the heart has its reasons, which reason knows nothing of." Then shaking his head as though waking himself from a trance, his gaze went back to Johnny. Drumming his fingers on the desk, he went on.

"Take time to think about it. But, remember that the offer won't last forever."

And Marcia won't wait forever, Johnny thought to himself.

"I'd be paying you. And It would be a lot more than the pay you're getting now.

Why not let that girl of yours decide if she'll wait another year or so? Or maybe she'd want to come over here. Just a thought," he added, shugging his shoulders.

"Anyhow, I've arranged for you to meet my nephew this afternoon. It's not far away. Just along by the new docks. He'll show you the plans and all that, and see what you think of each other. Oh, his name's Robert Hall, and he's called his new venture, 'R And J Hall Steamship Company.' You'll find it easy enough."
Getting up from his seat Johnny shook the older man's hand firmly,

"Thank you sir for the chance you are offering me. I'll give it a great deal of thought, for I'm tempted to take you up on it. I'll let you know in a couple of days."

"I told Robert that you'd be with him around two."

"But I'd need to get back to work," Johnny protested.

"Oh, don't worry about that. I'll send somebody down to tell Frazer you'll not be in this afternoon. When will you be seeing Mrs....er' Morris next?"

"I'm to go round to the newspaper to tell her what I thought of the article she wrote; when I've read it."

"Maybe she'd be able to help you with your decision, concerning my offer. She's a wise woman."
Johnny gave him a lopsided grin,

"think I'll do that."

"Good man. See you in a couple of days then."

When the door closed behind him, John Hall, sat staring out the window, a slight grin forming on his lips. He had made a start at impressing her. And it would be all to his advantage in the long run in spite of his ulterior motives.

Johnny Maloney was a smart young fellow, a good hard worker and obviously educated into the bargain. Just the fellow that his hot-headed, daydreaming nephew needed he decided, and he was nearly sure that he would accept.

He had often regretted not marrying and having children of his own. But, somehow no one ever matched up to Catherine in his eyes until it was too late. Now, after all his success and hard work, he had no child of his own to hand his business empire onto. He sighed deeply before going back to the outer office.

Walking along the crowded, busy docks Johnny's thoughts were on the offer of a lifetime that had just been made to him. He had grown strong and muscular in body from heavy work, and had matured in mind from boy to man in little more than a year. Yet his love for Marcia had not changed, rather it had become stronger, and he was terrified of losing her. Yet, he had also a compelling desire to be successful and prove himself. He walked past a beggar with his back against a wall, exhibiting scars and mutilations proclaimed by a placard hung about his neck, to be the result of shipwreck. Johnny ignored the rattling tin cup just as he ignored the street musician standing barelegged and bareheaded in the gutter, scraping at a fiddle. Two drunken seamen stammered and cursed over their possessions and a runner herded a family of frightened emigrants towards the doorway of a festering boarding house. The familiarity of the scene did not impinge on Johnny's consciousness as he searched for the sign proclaiming

'R And J Hall Steamship Company'.

Robert Hall wore spotless linen, a light grey suit and grey top hat. He had a trim fair moustache and spoke in a soft educated drawl that grated on Johnny's nerves.

'He doesn't intend to get his own hands dirty in this venture,' Johnny thought in his first summing up.

But, as the afternoon wore on, his opinions of Robert Hall changed and he knew that he had judged him too rashly. There was no doubting his knowledge of shipbuilding and steam in particular. Johnny was bowled over by his enthusiasm as he warmed to the young stranger. He spent a couple of hours alone in Robert's office studying the plans and by the end of the day he wanted to know every inch of the new ship; every plank of timber every nut and bolt. He had become so engrossed in the plans that, he failed to notice Robert Hall standing impatiently at the door waiting to lock up. When he finally tore himself away Robert remarked,

"I take it that you will be joining me." Johnny nodded.

"Can't wait"

"'Till tomorrow then."

Johnny walked for miles lost in deep thought. His plans to get home to Marcia had changed so suddenly, that it took even himself by surprise. And yet he was troubled.

He could not let his dream of marrying the girl he loved pass, and his dilemma deepened into near panic. Without hardly being aware of it he found himself outside the home of Catherine Morris. Walking up to the door, he pulled the bell and waited, then vaguely wondered what he was doing there. The same housekeeper answered the door and recognised him instantly.

"Good to see you again. Come on in," she urged opening the door wider. He hesitated,

"is Mrs. Morris at home?"

"She is."

"Do you think she'd have time to see me?"

"Sure she would," she said, standing aside to let him pass.

He sat in the same room and waited.

"Good to see you Johnny. I intended to go and see you tomorrow to tell you how well your newspaper story went down. Had lots of folks call at the paper to tell me how much they both enjoyed and learned from it. Many of them Irish immigrants themselves, who were glad that the people here learned something of their reasons for being here."

"The newspaper story's not why I'm here. I thought...hoped you might be able to advise me about something. Well...you know a bit about me. That's if it's not too much bother?"

"I'm only too pleased that I've found a friend in you, to cheer my loneliness---a friend who's brought me a glimpse of a different world, new interests, new problems, which if I can't cure at least I can alleviate a little."

When he had finished telling her about the golden opportunity he had been offered, she looked at him searchingly for a few seconds, before saying, "It's that girl of yours back home, isn't it? You just wouldn't be happy here without her."

"That's about it."

"Well Johnny. Let me try and think of a way around this. Have you asked her to come here and join you?"

"I hinted in a couple of letters. But she's got her father to think about. And, then there's wee Cassie O'Connor. She's a wee girl that was evicted...well, she's sort of adopted her as far as I can make out. And she writes to me too...wee notes inside Marcia's letters. She makes me feel as if she's a wee sister."

"Maybe she could take the child with her."

"Maybe. But, she has a mother that might not be agreeable."

"I still think that you should put the proposition to her. Send her your account of everything that's happened to you, and I'm willing to bet that she will come."

"How long will it take to build this ship?"

"Oh, about two years, or maybe more."

Looking away from his gaze, she said, "two years is a long time when you're in love. When she looked back at Johnny, her eyes were brimming with tears. It seemed as if all her pent-up loneliness had suddenly broken bounds and without warning overwhelmed her.

"I'm sorry," she muttered, regaining her composure. "If you need somewhere to live, my son will help out there. It's his department."

"Thanks for listening. I'll take your advice and see what happens," Johnny said, suddenly feeling as if a weight had been lifted from him.

Later at the door, Catherine Morris said suddenly,

"I must say John Hall's thoughtful gesture took me by surprise a little. And I had him marked down as a greedy business man. I must make a point of going round to thank him. He's made a good choice in you Johnny, of that I'm sure!"

Walking home Johnny formed the words of his letter to Marcia in his head. Quickening his pace he was determined to get the letter written before his enthusiasm seeped away.

Chapter 18

Donegal

When Cassie finished reading Johnny's letters she knew without being actually told that Marcia would go to Canada. Sick at heart, she stole upstairs to her room and curled up in bed, covering her head. Sometime later her mother called her for school, "I can't go. I'm sick, an' I've an awful headache," she muttered, not taking her head out from under the blankets. When Ellen went downstairs to make the breakfast, Cassie let all the pent-up tears flow uninterrupted.

Sometime later she became aware of Marcia sitting in the chair close to the bed.

"Thought you were sleeping Cassie."

"Are you going away...to be with Johnny?" Marcia didn't answer. She looked beyond her to the open window, her shoulders heaving. Her eyes, very heavy, very sorrowful met Cassie's unflinchingly,

"yes, Cassie. I must. You know I hate leaving you and my father. But, I can't mope 'round here forever."

"Have you told him?"

"Johnny?"

"No…your father."

"I told him last night." She gave a long low sigh before she said, "and that was as bad as telling you."

"Please take me with you. I'd work for you in Saint John. I'd keep your house clean, an' I'd wash Johnny's shirts…"

"Cassie stop it. I can't take you with me…you know I can't."

Raising herself up on one elbow, her eyes blazing, she yelled,

"go away an' leave me alone. I hate you. You promised you'd look after me. You promised," she screeched, her voice braking into uncontrollable sobs.

When the sobbing subsided Marcia said,

"Cassie please believe me when I say I wish there was another way."

"You said that you'd always look after me. Now you don't care what happens to me. Johnny's all you care about. I hate him, an' I hate you. Why can't you take me with you? Why?"

"Because, Cassie you belong with your mother. You're all she's left."

"She doesn't care about me. She wouldn't notice if I wasn't here."

"Oh, she would Cassie. I haven't the right to stand between you and your mother. She loves you too." As she looked at the despair in her eyes, Marcia wanted more than anything else to tell her that she had planned to take her to Canada. She hated that look of betrayal in her face. Reaching out she put her arms around her shoulders, and for a moment they clung like frightened, desperate children, not sure which way to turn. Then pulling away from Marcia, Cassie said with a mock show of defiance,

"don't tell me when you're going. For I won't say goodbye to you."

Marcia's ship sailed for Saint John on the twenty-ninth of May 1852, the day before Cassie's twelfth birthday. True to her word, Cassie didn't say goodbye to her friend and protector, staying well out of sight when the time came for Marcia to leave; so great was her grief and sense of betrayal.

From her bedroom window Cassie watched her leave in the trap, a sad and sombre Reverend by her side. It was a serene and beautiful May Day, the land smiling with summer promise, and the air rich with the scent of hawthorn. Glancing up at Cassie's window Marcia's heart felt like it had been turned to stone. Only her compelling love for Johnny drove her on, for her trial at leaving was a sore one.

Locking herself in her room, Cassie ignored her mother's pleas to come with her to the cottage. Her food sat outside the door untouched, while inside Cassie lay rigid, her tormented thoughts too deep for tears. She heard her mother leave through the back door, and a lonely stillness filled the space, as it dawned on her that she was alone in the big old house for the very first time. No matter what befell her she would have no one to comfort her, no one who really cared. Like an ice cold wave submerging her, came the realisation of her aloneness. She saw the ghost of the ship that would take Marcia away from Ireland, disappearing into the ocean mists and out of sight.

Through the open window the only sounds were the plaintive bleat of sheep on the hillside and the Blanack Water singing on the stones. As darkness fell the house began to creak and groan. She lay rigid, her ears picking up every new sound, that seemed to spell out sinister terrors from the growing shadows. As fear overtook her stubborn self pity, she jumped out of bed and bounded out of the house.

A young moon was rising, shy yet radiant, like a bride, over the solemn rim of the hills, when Cassie sped from her terrors to the little cottage, where Ellen, waiting anxiously at the door saw her coming. The relief she felt in that moment was immense, 'Lizzy was right when she made signs for me to wait just a bit longer,' she whispered. Then running to meet her she held out her arms. For a moment she seemed as though she might run into them, then thought better of it and walked on past her and into the kitchen.

Ellen lay listening to Cassie sigh and call out in a restless sleep. Marcia's leaving had affected her far more than she realised. Getting out of bed, she went over to where she lay, and as she watched her child, tossing and turning in her restless torment she was overtaken with guilt. She had to face up to having been guilty of not only ignoring her child, but actually resenting her. She was forced to confess to herself, that she resented her being here at all when Michael and her baby sons were gone. She had hoped that she had kept this fact secret from Cassie, but in her heart she knew that she hadn't. 'God, forgive me...I even resented the devotion that Michael showed you,' she whispered silently. The letter that Marcia had left for her lay unopened. She had listened at the door when Marcia told her she was leaving and heard Cassie beg her to take her with her. For a fearful moment she had waited for Marcia to tell the truth, that she wanted her to take Cassie with her but, that she her mother, had refused. As she stood there in the semi-darkness she knew that she must tell Cassie that her friend had not betrayed her, whatever the consequences; she owed her that much.

Before setting out for the Rectory, she sat Cassie down on the nearest chair and told her of her encounter with Marcia.

"You see I couldn't bear it if you went too. You are all I have left Cassie."

Cassie stared at her in a stunned silence. After a while a

few scalding tears filled her eyes, before she asked brokenly,

"why didn't you let me go? You never even notice me. You don't want me. Marcia was the only one that cared about me since Daddy died."

"That's not true. I do care about you...so very much. I know I've not been as good a mother as I should have. But I do love you."

"You should have let me go. You should have. You've hardly even spoke to me in two years." Looking away from her mother's stricken face, she looked around the bare kitchen noticing the strange shadows thrown by the early sunlight. She looked down and saw her bare feet, side by side, close together, on the earthen floor.

They looked very white, and somehow pathetic. Someday they will carry me, she thought, far away from here. As she ran towards the door, Lizzy appeared as if from nowhere, barring her way. Her mouth opened, and strange inaudible sounds seemed to come from a great distance. Her eyes blazed with anger as she pointed back towards the chair that she had just risen from, while Cassie stared back in blank astonishment. Overcome by fear of her, she felt she had no choice, other than to obey. Lizzy is jumping to my mother's defence, she thought in surprised bewilderment. Glancing at her mother again she was surprised to see tears streaming down her face, and at once felt pity stir in her.

Going over to where she sat, she put a reluctant arm

around her heaving shoulders,

"I'm sorry. I'll stay with you...for now," she said awkwardly. Turning to face her, Ellen patted her arm gently,

"thank you Cassie. I'll promise I'll do better. And if when you're old enough; you still want to go. Well then, so be it."

Later, when she finally read Marcia's letter she felt a little better and her heartache seemed somehow, more bearable. Marcia had not intended to abandon her after all. Her thoughts went back to her earliest memories. She remembered the time her wee brother died, and the sad, bewildered feeling she had. She remembered going over to sit on her weeping mother's knee and waiting for the comfort of her arm around her; but it never came.
Taking her diary out from under the bed she began to write.

Chapter 19

James Mahon

They sat outside the cottage on a warm August evening, Lizzy was spinning, Ellen sewing and Cassie doing her school work. Suddenly, he staggered towards them, and dropped in a huddled heap beside the spinning wheel. He had not been drinking. Ellen quickly made certain of that. He was exhausted by travel and hunger. His clothes were in tatters, the soles of his shoes worn through, the bare blistered soles of his feet clearly visible and the hollows in his gaunt cheeks told of sleepless nights and weary, hungry days. While staggering towards them there had slipped from his hand a few folded canvases, a box of paints, and a decapitated straw bag which flew open spilling out a few threadbare garments, a fragment of dry bread, and a few tattered books.

Although grimy and unshaven there was about him none of the hallmarks of a gypsy.

Between the three of them, they managed to get him inside and onto the bed in the kitchen. Ellen gave him sips of water and wiped his brow with a damp cloth and waited until, with a sigh, he opened his eyes. His lips were dry and cracked, his eyes dull.

"Where am I?" he inquired faintly.

"In good hands. Don't try to talk `till you're stronger."

"Who are you?" he asked, "How did I get here? Oh, it's coming back. I was looking...for shelter for the night. Walked for days... trying to get to Derry."

"Just lie and rest. You can tell us all about it when you're stronger. Lizzy's getting you a drop of broth. Looks like you could do with it," Ellen said, tucking a blanket around his bony frame.

It was another two days before he was strong enough to tell them his story. His name was James Mahon, he was a teacher and an artist, and he had walked all the way from a village in County Leitrim. When the potato crops failed for the second year in succession, between the fever and emigration, the hunger had virtually wiped out the entire village.

He had been on the road for weeks hoping to earn enough money as an artist to pay his passage to America.

"I thank you for your kindness. But I have no money to pay you. I'll be on my way in the morning," he concluded.

"You'll do no such thing. You stay here 'till you're strong again...then you can decide," Ellen said, ignoring his attempts at protest.

The remainder of August was warm and dry which helped James Mahon's recovery. His blistered feet had become infected, thus rendering him virtually immobile. And so he sat outside the cottage for a good part of each day soaking up the warm, late summer sunshine. Cassie gradually befriended the stranger and would sit outside close beside him each evening when her chores were done. At first they would sit in a comfortable silence, until gradually they began to communicate. He told her about his teaching and his work as an artist, that had gradually dried up, and about his hopes of finding new subjects in Derry that might pay for his passage to America. She warmed further to the stranger when, he began taking an interest in her school work, giving her help and encouragement and her earlier annoyance at having to give up her bed in the kitchen evaporated as the days passed.

When he told her one evening that he was well enough to be on his way again she felt an unexpected and overwhelming sadness.

It was remembering the conversation she had with the Reverend a few days earlier that sent her scurrying off in the direction of the rectory the following evening.

She hadn't missed a day at school since it opened. She worked hard at her lessons and filled in events of each day, however small, in her diary like she promised

Marcia. The small school house was now overcrowded as more and more children returned to school. 'It was a sign that maybe the worst of the famine was behind us,' the Reverend told her. "We hope to get a bigger school with two classrooms and another teacher very soon. That's what the board promised anyhow," he had said, a few weeks ago.

Reverend Briggs sat in his study staring gloomily out the window, the letter from Julia's sister still in his hand. He couldn't quite get his head around the fact that she was coming back into his life and that not even sisterly loyalty could tolerate Julia. But, he had to admit that, as his sister-in-law had pointed out, she was his responsibility.

He was now, more than ever convinced that his wife was mentally deranged, much as he hated to admit it and that somehow he must cope with it.

When he finally noticed Cassie standing in the doorway, he forced himself to smile.

"Oh, Cassie. I didn't see you there. Come in and sit down."

He looked gaunt and thinner than when she last saw him.

"I was just thinking about Marcia and how much I'm missing her," he said with a sigh. Then glancing at Cassie, he saw her eyes mist over, "you too eh?"
She nodded. "Maybe we'll feel better when we hear from her," he ended with a sad smile. "Anything else on your

mind?"

It was the opening she'd been waiting for. She told him all about James Mahon.

"He'd be a grand teacher for Glenscullion school. Do you think you could give him the job?" she ended.
He looked at her closely for a few seconds before he answered,

"firstly Cassie, it's not up to me. But, I can go and see him...then if I think he's qualified enough I could maybe recommend him. But don't you go giving him false hopes 'till we see." They exchanged a smile. Then looking absently into the distance, he sighed again before he said, "my wife's returning in a week or so. Just got a letter from her sister." Cassie's mouth opened wide in shock as she tried to contemplate 'the Madam's return.

The memory of her made her shudder. She would rather sit along the cold ditches, herding the cow that her mother had bought with her legacy; scrub the pots, clean out the stable, anything other than be at 'the Madam's beck and call again. Seeing the shock on her face, the Reverend said,

"oh, don't worry Cassie...I won't expect you to run around after her this time. She's bringing a maid with her it seems; though I doubt if she'll stay. I'll think of... something," he ended lamely.

James Mahon had agreed to wait until after the teaching post had been decided upon before moving on.

"I'd need to be doing something soon. Can't live off other people for much longer," he told Cassie.

"But, you can't work 'till your feet heal," Cassie reminded him.

He looked at her intently for a minute or so, before he said,

"tell you what. I'll paint your portrait. You have a very interesting face and the most amazing eyes.

Aye, it might even be my master piece." Cassie blushed deeply, before stammering,

"paint a portrait...of me?"

"Aye, a portrait of you. It's my way of saying thank you. An' like I said you're the perfect subject."

They were sitting outside the cottage, as the first few strokes of Cassie's portrait began, when Ellen came home from the Rectory that evening. The gloomy expression on her face, told Cassie that, she had found out about 'the Madam's return. She walked inside without a word or a glance in their direction. James Mahon's deep set eyes, as they fell on Cassie's face lit up marvellously, and the long fingers which held the brush moved swiftly and confidently on the canvas.

As he worked, he saw in his subject a fine face, nobly featured, but it had a sadness beyond her years, and in the deep set green eyes burned the sombre fire of one who dreamt dreams far beyond the sorrows of the time. Cassie's mind was on her mother's look of despair and in spite of her resentment of her mother, she felt sorry for her. And much as she had hated leaving the Rectory, she was bound to admit that dreary and dark as the cottage was, it was good to have a haven away from 'the Madam' when she returned.

When the light faded, James Mahon covered the canvas with an old rag, refusing to let Cassie have a peep,

"All in good time…all in good time," he repeated.

Cassie got her first letter from Marcia, on the same day that, the portrait was finished. When she arose the sun was shining through the open door. "Come and see," James Mason said, standing aside from where the portrait stood propped up against the back of a chair. Staring at it Cassie asked him,

" this really me?"

"It's you; as I see you."

He beheld her small, straight figure, dressed in a peculiar shapeless frock and he could see the beautiful woman that she would become. Looking back at him, she smiled,

"it's lovely. Thank you so… very much."

"You're welcome. And, thanks to you, I've been offered the teaching job. I start in September when the school opens. I must warn you, that I'm a cross teacher who will expect the best from everyone. You included."

"Right ye' are sir," she said, with a mock bow.

"Can I take the portrait down to show the Maloneys?"

"It's yours to do what you like with. Now I'll get back to weeding the potatoes."

With a wintry little smile he walked out towards the garden, his black felt hat perched at a right angle on his head. She had grown to like him in the few weeks since he staggered into their lives, and she knew that her mother liked him too. She had lain awake listening to them talk late into the night, and that her mother had become more cheerful and somehow, more alive since he came had not passed Cassie's notice. James Mahon's arrival was the only good thing that had happened in Cassie's life since Marcia left. When Harry wrote to tell her that he wasn't coming home in June for the school holidays her spirits plunged. He had chosen instead to spend most of his holidays at a new friend's house in Derry and was only to spend a week at home. Cassie hid her tears and disappointment as best she could. But she felt that he too, had let her down and her heart ached with sadness.

She had decided that, in order to preserve what little pride she had left, she wouldn't answer his letter and would ignore him when he did come home.

Cassie walked down the winding road towards Ballyneely, passing the high grey stone wall of Albertine Hall. Just as she passed the gate lodge, she heard someone calling her name. Molly Bradley, the postmaster's wife, waved her arms to gain her attention.

She was a heavy set woman, dressed in black, and with a face like some large suspicious bird, Cassie thought.

"I've a letter for you…from Canada. From 'Miss Marcia Briggs', it says on the back. I'll just sit myself down for a bit, `till you've read it. There's not a sinner in Ballyneely that doesn't want to know how herself an' young Johnny fared." With that, she sat down heavily under the wall and waited for Cassie to open the letter.

It was well known to Cassie, that Molly made everyone else's business her own and would stop at nothing to get news to pass on to the next person she met.

"Aye, everybody wants to know how she an' young Johnny fared. A grand girl, Marcia Briggs. An' I hear that, that hateful snoot, of a mother of hers is coming back." As she looked down at the moon face and beady eyes, Cassie knew that, there was no escape from opening the letter in her presence.

She pretended to read from it, in short stammering sentences, stating that she had just arrived and had no news as yet. To Cassie's relief she seemed to accept this version of the letter contents and quickly changed the subject, "I hear that the gentry are coming back to the hall. That's what…I found out."

"Who told you?" Cassie asked.

"Him," she said, nodding back in the direction of the gate lodge, "our new land steward." She shrugged in contempt, before going on, "a wee runt of a man. Thin as a snake an' no humour in him at all. An' if I was to sit for a week, he wouldn't as much as break the seal on the letters I bring him. Aye, I'll tell himself to deliver his post in the future. The last time I was here he wasn't in. That's how I found out about the gentry coming back. Well, the letter was sitting there an' I seen the crest on the top of it. I read it to pass the time you see," she ended, getting stiffly to her feet. "What's that ye got?" she asked, spotting the canvas under Cassie's arm.

"It's… my portrait. The new schoolmaster painted it."

"Let me see. She stared at the picture and then at Cassie, before saying, "not a bad likeness. Aye, not bad. Why ye could nearly be taken for a beauty in it. But like I always say. Beauty never boiled the pot, an ugliness never thickened it,"

When at last, she went on her way, Cassie's patience had all but run out. She quickly found a secluded spot behind a tree and sat down to read Marcia's letter in peace.

After reading the final page Cassie put the letter on her lap and sat thinking, for it had given her much to think about. She told her about the joyful reunion with Johnny and of their wedding plans. She told her about the kindness of the Morris family who had given her a temporary home and helped her find her way around the strange new city. Then she concluded. 'I miss you, my father and Henry more than words can say, and I look

forward to the day when we can all be together again.'
'You're loving friend Marcia.'

Cassie sat still, letting her thoughts drift away. She had crossed the Atlantic in her head, and had witnessed the joy of the lovers reunion; she had seen the great new city of their adopted country and how she wished that she could be there to share in it all. She got to her feet with a sigh and walked on down to the village.

John Murphy stood staring vacantly from the doorway of his shop. The only sounds were the bleating of goats and the sharp cr—omp---cr—omp of metal against metal coming from the direction of the forge. She could hear the creak of a loaded cart, and the rumble of wheels coming from the direction of the winding road that curved towards the river.

She left Murphy's shop carrying the few messages that her mother had ordered under one arm, and the canvas under the other and headed along the shore road towards Maloneys.

She trudged along the winding shore road lost in thought. When she rounded the bend at the top of the bray, she saw Harry standing still, silhouetted against the dark hills. Her heart leapt with joy at seeing him so unexpectedly, making her forget completely her earlier promise to ignore him. He ran towards her smiling broadly his eyes keen, yet pathetically wistful fixed themselves on her face.

The observed each other in silence, before he said,

"glad I caught up with you. Your mother said you'd come this way."

"Didn't think you'd bother to come at all," Cassie said sourly, remembering her promise to punish him.

"I was sorry after, that I agreed to stay in Derry. I didn't like it much."

"Don't expect me to feel sorry for you. Some best friend you turned out to be," she said, walking past him. "Anyway, I've made new friends now." He jumped past her again at speed, and turned to face her again, "please Cass...I'm sorry. You are still my very best friend, even if you have new friends."

Cassie stood looking at him in silence, noting the sad expression in his eyes and the lock of blond hair that fell across his forehead. He had grown taller, and looked somehow, more grown up.

"Can I come to the Malloneys with you? Please. The house was so lonely without Marcia, that I couldn't stay in it."

As she looked at him, her heart melted and with it her angry pride,

"all right. Come on then." He smiled at her and she smiled back.

They walked on around the narrow twisted road then, climbed up, onto the big flat rock at Dun Head where they had often sat before.

"I want to hear all the news...everything," he said,

looking down at her.

"If you'd come home when you should have you'd know everything long ago."

"I said I was sorry. I've still got two weeks. We can have great fun in that time."

Looking away from him, she threw a small rock into the sea and watched it splash as it hit the water. Her earlier anger and pride returning, she said,

"I won't have a lot of time to go about with you. I've made new friends from school. And there's the crowd at the crossroads dancing. I go there regular, you see," she added turning to face him again. The blue eyes that looked back at her, had a wounded look and, she watched them mist over before he looked away. He flicked back his yellow hair in embarrassment as he stared straight ahead.

Cassie immediately regretted her hasty words.

"But, the friends from school can wait. An' you can come with me to the crossroads."

Harry gave his attention to the western sky,

"looks like heaven's on fire," he hazarded.

"Wouldn't it be just our luck if it all got burned up 'fore we got there?"

He looked back at her again and now there was a grin on his face,

"you say the funniest things Cassie." Suddenly they both burst into laughter; all that went before, forgotten.

As they dandered slowly along the rutted laneway that led to Malloneys house, they planned the coming days. Cassie told him about her encounter with Molly, and about how she had read the land steward's letter, telling her about the return of the gentry to the Hall.

"She must have told all the village about it by now. For when I was in Brian's shop, I overheard them talking about it." Cassie went on, "Old Murphy said, they were nothing short of parasites. Parasites are fleas an' heather ticks, an' that...aren't they?" Harry regarded her amusedly, before nodding,

"aye that's about what they are. Hope they come before I have to go back to school."

"Why?"

"Well, then we could sneak in and get a look at them...see if they do look like fleas." Cassie looked up at him indulgently and giggled,

"I know how to get in through the wall. I did tell you about the time I stole the plums from the garden?"

"That's what give me the idea. An' there might be more plums into the bargain," he added, with a grin. They skipped along for the last few yards to the Malloneys' door.

A few days later Harry came to the cottage to find Cassie. His expression looked troubled as they walked after the cow down the lane. Herding the cow was one of Cassie's jobs each day, and since his return Harry came with her for company.

"What's wrong.? You look as if you lost a penny an' found a farthing," she said, as they sat down along the ditch.

"My mother's coming home tomorrow. And I've got to go back and help get the house ready."

"We've all got to do some work Harry."

"Oh, it's not that. My father says she's ill. It's in her head he says."

"Does he mean... sort of insane?"
He nodded solemnly,

"that must be what he means."
Cassie absently drew lines in the dirt, before she spoke,

"I'm... sorry. You know I never got on with her. But, still, I'm sorry she's sick."

"She's my mother and I've always been... sort of afraid of her too. Her sister's coming with her an' some sort of companion...an' maid."
Cassie gave a low whistle, before asking,

"will there be room for all them?"

"My Aunt's not staying...or only for a night or two. She'd lived with three different relations since she left home. But nobody could live with her. So they sent her back to my father. In the letter my Aunt said, she is my father's responsibility."

"Did the Reverend let you read the letter?"

"Well not...exactly," he said sheepishly, "I just wanted to know what's going on. So I read it."

"You mean you did a Molly the postmistress on it!"

she added, reprovingly.

"My aunt mentioned something about insanity. She said she couldn't bear her to go to an Asylum an' that my father has to take responsibility for her."
Looking at his troubled face Cassie's sympathy went out to him.

"Come on, the cow's eaten enough grass for today. I'll help you with the getting ready for your mother. Then tomorrow we'll go to the Hall like we said."
Glancing at him she noted that his eyes held that sorrowful expression, that always tore at her heart.

The Wordsworth poem that James Mason often quoted, when remembering the sorrows that the famine had wrought in County Mayo, kept repeating around in her head.

'There is a comfort in the strength of love;
'T will make a thing endurable, which else
Would overset the brain, or break the heart....'

They hunted the cow back to the small enclosure, then went on to the Rectory to begin the cleaning in readiness for the invasion from afar.

It was a misty morning with low cloud hanging around the hills when they set of to walk the two miles to Albertine Hall. Harry felt a sense of nervous excitement as desire for adventure surged up through his being, taking his mind away from his mother's impending arrival.

Cassie quickly found the gap in the high stone wall again.

Once on the other side of the wall, they walked along the path with noiseless feet. The path was dark and the trees looked very tall. They shut out the light and Harry remembered ghosts and goblins and bad fairies as they walked along. Reaching the garden gate, they hid behind the rambling rose and watching the gardeners as they worked. Cassie's spirits fell a little when she saw the plum trees bared of their fruit. They walked on in silence through the monkey-puzzles, and found a secluded spot behind a tree overlooking the front of the Hall. The sun began to make an appearance from behind the clouds. They talked in whispers as they rested, propping their backs against the tree. To the right Harry could just make out what looked like apples hanging from a tree close to the garden wall.

"I'm going to see if I can get a few apples," he said, scurrying off before Cassie could stop him. With her heart thundering in her ears, she watched him clamber up the tree in full view of the house.

With relief she watched him climb down from the high branches finally reaching the safety of the ground. But, her relief was short lived. In the distance the sound of wheels on the gravel and the snorting sounds of horses filtered through the air. Panic stricken, she stood up and waved her arms with a fury in Harry's direction. When he saw her he stooped down and dashed back to the seclusion of the tree trunk, just as the coach appeared. It swept around to the front steps and came to a halt. The footman opened the door, turned down the folding steps and helped first one and then another young woman alight, followed by a youngish man. The women stood smiling, their full skirts almost reaching the yellow gravel. Dressed in black, the housekeeper hastily descended the steps to greet them, while white capped maids stood demurely at either side of the entrance, leading to the open front door.

They watched them climb the steps and disappear behind the great oak door, and after them came a seemingly endless procession of luggage, carried by two men.

"They didn't look much like fleas or heather ticks to me," Cassie said, her thoughts on the elegant young women with their ruffling taffeta's. She sighed softly before saying wistfully, "wouldn't it be wonderful to be rich like them. To have beautiful clothes an' servants, an' carriages an' mansions."

"If I ever get rich Cassie, I'll buy you a mansion."

Turning around, she looked at him. He lay stretched out on his stomach, a long blade of grass hanging from his mouth, the lock of yellow hair hanging across his forehead. As she looked at him, sound, scent and feeling seemed on a different plane and had nothing to do with reality. She wanted them to stay here forever; just the two of them and the intense feeling of affection towards him scared her.

Knowing that they had only a matter of days left to enjoy together lay between them, heavy as doom. Delving into his pockets he handed her a pear,

"it was a pear tree after all. I nearly forgot about them."

Cassie bit into it and her teeth stuck solid in the tough hard flesh. When she finally dislodged it she said,

"it's as hard as hickory. Not ripe at all."

"Sorry. Poor Cass. Hope it didn't break your teeth. They looked good from the distance." Coming closer, he asked, "show me your teeth?" Baring her teeth for inspection, she watched him move his head from side to side, to get a better look.

Finally he gave a nod of satisfaction, "don't think there's any of them broke."

His eyes took on a wistful look as he gazed deeply into her eyes. Then he smiled that, appealing, crinkley smile, and in that moment he lit a lamp in her heart that was never to die. Then suddenly she was that insecure, lonely and frightened little girl again. 'Everyone I have ever loved and relied on has let me down,' an inner voice whispered. Panic mounted swiftly. She thought about her father, Marcia, and the coldness of her mother, the dark cottage and the grey walls of the workhouse. She was alone again in a frightening, dark world and she trembled with apprehension.

"What's wrong? Are you sick?" Harry asked, with urgency in his voice. She shook her head, glancing at his troubled expression, she said,

"It's just that you will go back to that school an' forget all about me. Then you'll go away to somewhere else...like Marcia did. She rubbed her hands up and down the rough warm trunk of the tree, before going on, "my father was the only one that really cared about me... an' he's gone."

They stared at each other in the shadow of the tree. Harry plucked a leaf from above his head and rolled it absently in his hands.

"Marcia left me too, you know. And, then there's my mother. I don't even want to see her." He threw away the leaf and gazed into space, before he added, "but, my father will make me go an' see her."

When he next looked at Cassie, she could see tears in his eyes. She pressed her fingers hard into the hole in the tree trunk. Her own self pity forgotten, she impulsively bent across and kissed him on the cheek.

"I'll go with you to see your mother... if you want me to?"

"Oh, would you?" She nodded.

"Thanks Cassie. Let's make a pledge under this tree."

"What'll we pledge?"

"We'll pledge to meet here again when we're grown up. Let's see I'm ...fourteen now. Let's say when I'm twenty an' you're nineteen."

"That's seven years away. Will I not see you for

seven years?" Cassie asked mournfully.

"Sure you will. But here in this place, on this day, in seven years," he repeated, holding out his hand, "shake on it." They shook hands and Harry kissed her on the tip of the nose. Jumping to his feet he ran to the edge of the lake, picking up and then discarding flat stones until he found a sharp one. Back at the tree he began carving first, Cassie's and then his own initials. Standing back he viewed his work with a nod of satisfaction. "Now, you carve the date," he said to Cassie, handing her the stone. With difficulty, Cassie pushed the sharp edge of the stone deeply into the bark and recorded the date. "Now, spit on your hand and we'll shake again. That's what we do at school when we make a bargain that we want kept," he hastily explained. When she had done as he asked, they shook hands firmly,

"I'll learn how to cook an' sew an' do all the lovely, fine darns that Lizzy can do...so I can look after you well, when you're grown up."

Getting stiffly to their feet again their soundless feet walked back along the dark pathway and out through the hole in the big grey wall and into the warm sunshine.
They slid into the rectory kitchen unnoticed. Ellen and Lizzy looked agitated as they prepared the evening meal for the new arrivals.

"Come on Cassie. I've been waiting for you to show up. We need all the help we can get."

"But, we're starving with hunger," Cassie protested.

"Serves you right, for gallivanting all morning." Then getting two bowls from the cupboard, she said, "come on both of you. There's a bit of soup left from lunchtime. Then you'll have to get to work. Your father was looking for you Harry. Your mother's back. She's upstairs. Your aunt's in the drawing room with your father." Harry's hunger seemed to vanish and was replaced by feelings of anxiety as he listened to Ellen's news. He had half hoped that, somehow, his mother might have changed her mind. He ate half the soup and went into the dark shadowy hall. From the direction of the study he could hear voices and he went closer to listen.

"I have told you that I'm accepting responsibility for her. The decision to go to you was entirely her own I assure you."

"She told us that you treated her abominably; that you incited the children against her, encouraged Marcia in an association with that unsuitable young man she has now run off to be with. I'm not saying that the way...she is now is all your fault because she was always difficult. But, you must bear some responsibility."

"I am not shirking my responsibilities. And, I must tell you that you listened to untruths and only half truths. I did not treat Julia badly at any time during our very difficult marriage. And as for our children...she brought that on herself.

Did she tell you that she befriended an evil man who had wrecked havoc on an already devastated people. And that she arranged for Marcia's young man to be arrested and deported like a criminal. Or, that she terrorised young Harry by threatening to have him sent back to that boarding school that nearly cost him his life. I could go on. But, I think you might have got the picture by now."

"I'm sorry Henry. I shouldn't have misjudged you. God knows, she's been a trial to us all these past months. I suppose I was just looking for someone to blame; something to account for...it. But I may as well say it. She's insane Henry."

Harry shuddered, and moved away from the door on tiptoe, to hide in the dark cupboard under the stairs, where he had always gone in times of trouble.

After a while his heart lightened a little and he crept out quietly to be confronted by his father as he came out the study door.

"Glad I caught you Harry. I want you to go up and see your mother before dinner.
She's not...too well. And you mustn't take too much notice of what she says. It's just her illness. Now off you go."

"I want Cassie to come with me," he said, his lower lip trembling.

"All right. But go up now. She's been asking for you."

Standing outside his mother's door, Harry felt sick and his mouth felt dry. Turning to face Cassie, who gave him a smile of encouragement, he gave a short knock at the door. They heard a muffled response and went in.
She lay on the couch by the window and it was as if she had never been away.

"Harry my darling," she said, excitedly, "how I've missed you. Come and give your mother a big hug." Glancing again at Cassie, he went slowly towards her and she clasped him tightly to her, "my darling boy," she repeated over and over. Then suddenly, she spotted Cassie standing in the shadows by the door and her face became contorted with rage. "What's that...that, creature doing here? Get her out. Get her out," she yelled, getting to her feet. Opening the door, Cassie looked at Harry,

"I'll wait outside," she said, her face reddened with fear. When she had closed the door behind her, Julia became calm again for a minute or so. Then suddenly she looked at Harry with a wild, hysterical stare in her eyes, "they're trying to poison me. I want you to watch all my food...every bit of it... to make sure they put no poison in it." Her lips drew together, her eyes veiled and her finger nails dug into the soft flesh of his arm. He felt a sharp bitter despair shoot through him, as the meaning of his mother's insanity sunk home.
Then mercifully, the woman who was hired as her companion came in carrying a tray

"I've brought your dinner. Thought that you'd

rather eat in your room…for tonight at any rate."

"I won't eat a bite. You won't poison me that easy."

"You know very well that nobody wants to poison you Julia."

"Prove it then. I won't touch a bite 'till you've tasted everything first."

Taking a spoon from the tray, she ate small samples from each dish.

"Satisfied?"

"Very well. I'll eat it."

When she began to eat, Harry made his escape unnoticed.

Outside the door Cassie still waited. They walked out of the house in silence and headed towards the shore. They sat on a flat rock and stared fixedly out to sea. A liner made its way slowly around the headland, looking majestic in the glow of the evening sun.

"I wish I was on that ship," Harry said, his voice breaking, "Marcia shouldn't have went away and left us." Suddenly he laid his head on Cassie's shoulder, and although she couldn't see his face she sensed he was crying. He hoped she wouldn't ask him why and after a while he remembered that he was grown up, and he got to his feet, walked away picking up pebbles and firing them into the water.

Harry dutifully visited his mother every morning during the following week, while Cassie waited outside the door.

Some days Julia appeared almost normal, and on other occasions agitated and frightening. When this ordeal was over they would walk back to the cottage where James Mahon would be waiting with freshly made potato bread hot from the griddle. On good days they would eat it outside while James smoked his clay pipe and dispensed his wisdom. Then they would herd the cow along the laneways to eat the late summer grass. They would herd the cow along grass covered, rutted laneways where empty desolate cottages that had once housed families stood vacant and forlorn. Doors creaked on their hinges, stools sat by empty hearths in the rush to escape the hunger. In the evening Cassie would go into the low, thatched barn and milk the cow, while Harry sat on the wee stool at the door with the silence full of small evening sounds; rustlings in the straw, the laboured breathing of the cow, the distant voice of a ship out in the bay, the chill winds that would creep over the fields as the tide turned. And at night before sleep overtook her Cassie recorded these events evocatively in her diary.

Chapter 20

7 Years Later

Cassie O'Connor had to bend low in order to slide through the small opening in the garden wall that she had slid through with such ease seven years earlier.

There was no sound to be heard. Cassie's muffled footsteps were amplified by the quietness as she made her way along the darkened pathway under the monkey puzzles. She found the oak tree and ran her fingers along the carving that Harry and herself had gouged into the trunk. 'Would he turn up? or would he even remember?' she wondered.

The sun appeared from behind the clouds as she sat down underneath the shady seclusion, letting her thoughts drift back over the past seven years. She was glad that she got here early. She wanted time to sit still and collect her thoughts. Her mind appeared to her as a kaleidoscope that had been so shaken by the changes in her life, it could not regain its original pattern.

It was five years since she last saw the Hall when she had walked up the front steps with James Mahon, the time he had been commissioned to paint the mistresses portrait. They had gone up the wide sweeping steps, James pulled the bell rope and they waited. When the butler answered he said,

"I'm James Mahon the artist and this is my assistant Cassie O'Connor. Your mistress is expecting us." They followed him through the spacious hall with its mosaic floor and were shown into an enormous room with chandeliers hanging from the ceiling, portraits lining the walls and enormous oak furniture. Cassie remembered how she had stood in awe at the splendid grandeur of it all and tried to contrast it with the dark dreary cottage they and almost everyone she knew lived in. When the mistress finally appeared she had been thunderstruck to hear James Mahon say,

"this room won't do at all Madam. The light is wrong in here. I need a room at the front of the house to work in; a room facing south."

"Brennan will arrange it, and show you where to go," she said, pulling the bell rope before disappearing again.

Looking at him opened mouthed Cassie said,

"I thought that she would show us the door when you said that. An' you didn't take off your hat neither."

Giving her a wry smile he said, "I'm an artist Cassie. An' as for taking off my artists cap. No, I don't do that for anybody. An' I only bow to my maker." He looked away from her for a few seconds. When he looked back at her again his eyes had misted over revealing a deep sadness within. "I've seen a lot of death and suffering over these past few years. I stared death in the face myself. I asked to be spared because I wanted to go on living...life was still precious. But I wasn't afraid. Cassie hear me. Always believe in yourself. And believe that you're as good, if not better, than the next person. I never read anywhere in the Bible where it says 'God bless the squire an' his relations, an' keep us in our proper stations.'

This famine is all but over. But we will never be the same nation again and in two hundred years from now this time will be remembered not only by the peoples of Ireland, but, by the descendants of our people who've been scattered to the four corners of the earth." As she listened Cassie promised herself that she would try to remember word for word of what he said, and write it down when she got home.

Later in the even bigger and even more luxurious room the portrait began to take shape. She had observed the posing mistress closely during the many sittings; she noted her hooked nose and small red rimmed eyes; every feature and flaw were etched on her brain forever. That was why the finished portrait became such a shock to her.

"That's not like her at all," she had said to James Mahon when he showed it to her just as they were about to deliver it, "you've made her look beautiful when she's really anything but."

"Ah, you're right Cassie. But if I painted her the way she really is she'd throw it back at me. Then I wouldn't get paid. No, she doesn't want an image of herself the way she really looks. So...I give her what she wants; I get paid an' everybody's happy."

They were shown into the same room that James Mahon had rejected on the first day, and waited for the mistress. They heard the swish of her skirts come from the direction of the hall.

"I'm quite beside myself with excitement. I can't wait to see my portrait." With a quick flick of his wrist James removed the cover and propped it up on a chair for inspection. Cassie watched closely as she stepped backwards for a better look. Nodding in their direction she said, "yes. I'm pleased with it. An excellent likeness. Excellent indeed."

Later handing James the money she said, "I've added a little extra for your child."
Well out of sight of the Hall, they had sat down while James counted his payment,

"a guinea extra. She's given you a guinea. 'Let joy be unconfined'," he said, looking at Cassie with a broad grin on his face. "A little deception pays off, eh'?"

"What'll I do with a whole guinea? Should I spend it all now or save it case there's another famine?"

"That decision's yours Cassie. Just do what you think is best with it. Them boiled sweets in Mick's shop looks tempting; what do ye think?"

Now standing alone looking at the big mansion before her, the memory of James Mahon's words gave her strength and comfort.

She thought back to the day two years ago when her mother told her that she was going to marry James Mahon. She had neither been shocked, nor surprised by this announcement. Her mother had told her about the coming event in embarrassed, faltering tones. "We both need companionship. And, as he was living here anyway...we decided that we might as well. We are good friends you see." Cassie had let her carry on with these explanations, faking a shocked silence. She was glad that they had each other and in a way it had relieved Cassie of the burden of responsibility for her mother. Their relationship was strained and somehow, she felt closer to James Mahon and it was to him that she confided her innermost thoughts. As she looked back over the years since he came into her life, she realised that she owed him much. He had encouraged, and sometimes bullied her into gaining that much prized scholarship for teacher training, and she glowed with pride remembering her successful examination results that meant she was now a trained teacher.

'I'm independent of everyone from now on; even Marcia,' she told herself. Thoughts of Marcia, brought back the memory of when she saw her, only yesterday. It was strange to see her back at the rectory after all this time and when she answered her knock at the big front door, time seemed to have jumped backwards.

"Cassie I've been waiting for you. Let me look at you," she said, stepping backwards to get a better view. "I always knew that you would turn out to be the beautiful, intelligent young woman that you now are. I will always remember the day you met us at the quayside last year. If you hadn't been standing beside my father, I don't think I'd have recognised you. Johnny was as anxious as me to see you…I told him so much about you." Her eyes lit up with pride before she asked, "was Johnny as you imagined him?"

Cassie smiled before she answered,

"No. He is far more charming an' better looking than I thought he'd be. You know Marcia; I didn't understand back then why you left. I felt so betrayed. I saw you as the one human being I really trusted. Then you were gone and I felt so betrayed…so alone. But now I understand why you had to go. But, I'm glad you're back."

"Thanks Cassie…thanks for understanding. Leaving you behind was the only regret I had about leaving."

"How's wee Kate?" Cassie asked, lightning the mood.

"She's grand. She's the image of her father. I only see Johnny on Saturday nights and Sunday forenoons." She sighed deeply before saying, "I miss our life in Canada. But Johnny's happy enough with his new shipbuilding contract. It's going to be a big vessel; the likes of which will not have been seen before. At any rate that's what he tells me. He was so fortunate in finding friends in Saint John who helped him to study shipbuilding. They were all so good to us both and because of them Johnny has found his true vocation. It's strange to say it. But, the cruel deed my mother did, brought some good."

"What about your mother? How is she?"
Marcia shook her head slowly,

"no change. Getting worse if anything. You know Cassie, it was Johnny who insisted that I come home to look after her. After all she did to him. I couldn't be that forgiving...I just couldn't."

"Does she remember what she did?" Cassie asked.
Marcia shook her head,

"if she does, she's making a good job of hiding it. When he's here she smiles at him like he was heaven sent. But, his willingness to forgive her has always amazed me."

Later they went upstairs to the nursery and gazed in fondness at the sleeping infant,

"she's like a wee angel. You are truly blessed Marcia," Cassie remarked. Then going over to the window she stared down at the driveway remembering the first time she set eyes on Harry, long ago in the midst of that thunder storm.

"Heard anything from Harry?" she asked, trying to sound casual, while her heart thundered in her ears.

"Nothing lately. He said he was coming home for a few weeks; but wasn't sure when."

Cassie wasn't sure whether Marcia's answer brought her fresh hope or despair as they said their farewells on the doorstep.

Chapter 21

Under The Oak

Now seated under the tree she wondered what she would do if Harry didn't turn up. She had to face it, he may have forgotten all about his promise of seven years ago. She had only seen him twice in the intervening years and when he kissed her goodbye and smiled his familiar crinkly smile, it was enough to leave the lamp in her heart trimmed and bright until his next letter came. She had known for a long time that she loved him; a love that began in childhood. There had been other suitors that she had entertained only but briefly; none matching up to Harry.

As the minutes ticked past, her thoughts became jumbled and frantic letting her old feelings of insecurity and inadequacy creep back to haunt her. Overhead the sky began to darken and become heavy mirroring the heaviness in her heart. In adulthood, Harry probably thought her a very poor bargain and no match for the educated son of a clergyman. And what would his father say about the prospect of the penniless, homeless child of a dead fisherman whom he had helped to rescue from the workhouse as a match for his son? She knew that his father had been disappointed when Harry chose medicine instead of the church. Cassie knew he would make a fine doctor who would serve humanity well and she had been delighted when he wrote and told her of his decision. Scalding tears filled her eyes and she roughly swiped them away, desperately trying not to let her tears break through the steel of her pride. The shattering blow of this realisation came unexpectedly, making everything seem unreal. 'I've been such a fool,' she repeated silently to herself.

Getting stiffly to her feet, she was about to walk away when she heard the carriage wheels on the gravel, just as she and Harry had done seven years earlier. Hiding behind the tree again, she watched as the footman lowered the steps and the gentry stepped down onto the yellow gravel. She mentally willed them inside the big door so she could run as fast as her legs could carry her through the dark monkey puzzles, and escape with her grief.

She watched the last full skirt finally disappear inside the door, before she finally made a move towards the path just as a streak of lightning split the darkening sky.

A short distance along the path she heard him call her name,

"Cassie. Cassie."

Turning around she saw him standing under the tree, a lock of hair hanging limply across his forehead. As he came towards her a long brilliant flash of lightning lit up the space between them.

"I thought you weren't coming…that you'd forgot."

"I couldn't get through our hole in the wall," he said, panting breathlessly. "Forgot that I've grown a bit in the last seven years. I went to the big gates instead just as the carriage come through. Then I had to hide. I was terrified I'd be too late an' you'd be gone." Holding out his hands he walked towards her and they clasped their hands together. He stared at her for a long moment before he spoke. "Cassie. My beautiful green eyed Cassie." Then lifting bodily into his arms and swung her around until she felt dizzy. Back on her feet again she swayed sideways and giggled, "I wanted you to laugh. I wanted to see if you still had that gap between your teeth. And you have. Every time I felt lonely or bothered over the years I would close my eyes and picture you. I would hear you laugh and see your dancing green eyes and just the thought of you would make all seem well again.

Then he flung his arms around her and hugged her, then stood back for inspection, "You look so…so beautiful and grown up. I've missed you. God I really have."

Then bending down he cupped her face in his hands and kissed her at first, softly and then urgently on the lips. Cassie's legs felt like jelly as she tried desperately to make sense of this strange feeling. She looked at his handsome, honest face and remembered the little boy who cried on her shoulder; the friend she had shared her hopes and fears with.

The rain began to come down in a deluge and they ran for cover towards the summer house at the edge the lake. They sat silently on the wooden bench with their arms around each other, before Harry said, "When I graduate in June, I would like to go to Canada to practice medicine. For a few years at any rate."

Cassie felt her spirits sink. 'Has he no plans for me in his life after all?' she asked herself silently. Then she heard him say, "But I'll only go if you come with me. I want to marry you. You're the only girl I've ever loved.

"Would you come to Canada with me? Oh, please say you will. I want to go to Saint John in New Brunswick where Marcia and Johnny were. So many of the famine victims fled there and I know I'd find work." Looking closely into her eyes with an anxious frown he added, "it's all right if you don't want to go. I'll stay here...just as long as we can be together."

"I'll go anywhere with you. Timbuktu even!"
He looked full into her eyes again, and in his own she read a look of love which sent her heart racing with joy. As the lightning lit up the sky, Cassie felt sure that she would never feel afraid or insecure again.

Cassie awoke from a dream filled sleep and blinked

suddenly remembering the day that it was. She felt excited and sad all at the same time. Cassie saw the future in a series of flashes, startling moments so brief that they could arrest a moment in mid air. Memory of the night before came to her now. The music still sounded in her head. It had been a night in her honour; a night of joy and sadness that mingled together like the cloud and brief glimpses of sunshine of a Donegal sky. It was her farewell night. In two days time she and Harry would be on a ship sailing to New Brunswick. She felt excitement well up at the thought of this new challenge and overwhelming joy at the thought of being with Harry on that journey together. But, tears now welled up from within at the thought of parting.

Memory of the conversation she had with her mother the night before came back clearly. She had summonsed her to the upper room half way through the evening.

They both sat on the bed that she shared with James Mahon, a flickering candle casting its shadows on their faces.

"Cassie I have something I want to give you," she began. "Your father gave it to me the evening before our wedding. It's just a wee locket. I know he'd want you to have it."

"I couldn't take it Mammy. He gave it to you."

"I don't need anything to remember him by....it's all here," she said putting the flat of her hand on her heart. "And anyway, if anything happens to me you might not get it and it's rightfully yours."

Cassie could feel her throat tighten as her words sank in. 'I might never see her again...never see any of them,' seemed to scream out silently inside her head. Up to this moment she had consoled herself with having a joyous homecoming in the not too distant future.

"We won't be gone forever. We'll be back again in a few years," she said, in as firm a voice as she could manage.

Ellen gave a long low sigh before saying,

"I hope so Cassie. But I'm not getting any younger... an' who knows. I have wanted to try and explain why I have been less of a mother... than I should have been. You've had it hard pet and I've been to blame. When I...we lost your father I didn't want to go on. And, for some reason I kinda blamed you for being here and him gone. Every time I looked at you I felt like that, for a long time after. Maybe because you're a mirror image of him." She shook her head from side to side, before burying her face in her hands. Cassie could feel her shoulders shake and knew that she was sobbing silently. She could feel her pain like the blade of a sharp knife sinking into her chest. Reaching out she put her arms around her shoulders, rocking her gently for a few seconds before she spoke.

"It's all right. I hold no grudge an' I'll be back before you know it."

"Aye Cassie. I know...I know. But you see I've seen so much death an' parting that I sort of expect it now. My heart has hardened and I try to ward off pain nowadays. But, I've been luckier than most. Do you know Cassie, if we'd gone into that workhouse I'd never have come out of it again. There was no will left to live." Cassie shuddered as she remembered only last week when she had stood outside the workhouse and watched old people shuffling along the paths like shadows, whispering courage to themselves and clutching their crooked walking sticks. In her heart she had to agree that death would have been better.

Ellen's voice broke into her thoughts again.

"I know Harry will be good to you and look after you. He's a kind decent lad. I don't know if you've come to any arrangement about your wedding. I mean... your different religions. All I want to say about that is think it over well, and make sure that neither of you regret any decisions you make. It will be easier getting married away from Ireland. You will be free to make the decisions without interference."

"I'll miss you. If you didn't have James Mahon I wouldn't be leaving you," Cassie said, turning to face Ellen.

"Aye, James is very good for me. But your father was the only real love in my life. An' he's still with me, helping me along the way. Considering everything we've not done so bad... you and me. We must have had a guardian angel somewhere.

They could hear the fiddler strike up a jig, its lively cheerful notes lightning the air of sadness between them. "Come on we'll go back and we'll dance. Aye, dance to your future."

Over the heads of the dancers Cassie saw him standing in the doorway. Their eyes met and he smiled his lopsided grin. Pushing back his lock of blonde hair he came towards her with his arms held out,

"dance with me green eyes?" She nodded, and they danced around the earthen floor to the ever quickening rhythm of the music.

Later they walked together along the familiar laneway and watched the moon drift in and out of the clouds. "I hope that you won't be too homesick Cassie. But if you are... I want you to know that I'll take you back."

"So long as we're together I'd go anywhere," she said, reassuringly.

Remembering the feel of his kisses made her sigh with longing. Any earlier regrets swept suddenly away.

The Reverend, Ellen, James Mahon, Marcia and Maggie stood in a row at the dockside making idle stiff conversation as they waited. Harry and Cassie stood silently a little distance from them, their faces looking strained and pale in the yellow evening light. Finally, it was time to board the ship that would take them to far off

Saint John in New Brunswick. The Reverend stepped forward and embraced them in turn, "may God bless and keep you both from harm," he said, in a broken voice.

When the goodbyes were said they walked towards the gangplank, they could hear the sounds of grief all around them, and a part of each of them wanted to turn around and go back. But they carried on climbing aboard, each step feeling as heavy as their hearts.

They stood on the deck gripping the rail with clenched fists, the sounds of the crying now drowned out by the strains of a lament from a solo fiddle player. Gulls slid through the air above them as white as drifting ashes, and the water dabbled softly on the side of the ship as it began to move slowly away from the dock.

Harry drew a long, unsteady breath and without taking his eyes off the point on the dockside on which they were fixed, he laid his hand palm up, on the rail. Cassie put hers into it. And as though he had not really expected this, he turned to face her and found that she was smiling. She leaned a little towards him, her fingers tightening on his,

"it'll be all right love," she whispered.

"I know. It'll be more than all right," he said kissing her softly on the forehead.

"We are far luckier than most. We have the Morris' to meet us an' help us 'till we get the hang of the place," Cassie added, as the ship moved further and further away on out to the open sea.

Hazel Mc Intyre

Chapter 22

Donegal 1995

Mary Thompson sat gazing out the window towards the distant hills, then brought her attention back to the word processor. She had begun working on the last chapter and was finding the task difficult. Re-reading her work from the previous day, she pressed the delete button with a sigh. Picking up one of the diaries again, she opened a page at random and read again Cassie's poignant account of meeting Harry under the tree by the lake at Albertine Hall. She was about to begin writing again when she had an idea. Getting her coat from the hall stand she grabbed her car keys and went outside. She stood in the driveway gazing at the cottage that had been her home for the past fourteen months. The winter had been cold and bleak, but the walls of the cottage were stout, and she had a good oil heating system and blazing turf fires to keep out the chill. New York and her career seemed a million miles away right now. Occasionally while watching TV or reading the newspaper the world from her past intruded and seemed alien to the world she now inhabited. At times she felt as if she were in a time machine, drifting in and out of past and present. She stopped the car in front of Sara McLaughlin's bungalow, got out and knocked on the door. Sara had been a friend and lifeline to her during the past months, helping her as if she had been a older sister.

"Mary, good to see you. Come in, come in," she said holding the door open.

"Haven't time today Sara. Got a bee in my bonnet. I want to go to the old Hall...read about it in the diaries you see. And I thought it might help me to make a better job of the last chapter of the book."

"I'll soon direct you. But, there's not much left of it. We used to play up there when we were waines. Aye, it must have been a grand place in its day."

"How long since it was last lived in?"

"Oh, let me think. Way back in the early forties I believe. The last lord of the manor had two daughters. One was drowned in the south of France. The younger daughter married a no good they said. He gambled away everything and then disappeared with some Spanish woman he met in London. She lived on in the Hall 'till she died following a fall in the garden. Some other distant relations of the Simms family inherited it I believe. He's never been near the place. Just rents out the land to a local farmer."

"Thanks Sara. You're a mind of information."

"I'm waiting patiently to read this book when it's finished. How long more will it take?" she asked with a broad grin.

"Nearly finished it. And, I'm nervous as a kitten. It's my tribute to Cassie O' Connor and to all the Irish people who lived and died during that tragic time in our history. But, if my grandmother approves of my effort...then that's all I'll ask."

Sara smiled encouragingly, before saying,

"she'll approve. Every time I go to see her, she talks non stop about you and your gift for the written word. She has so much tenderness in her voice when she talks about you."

Mary thought about the meaning of that rare thing 'tenderness'. A quality different from kindness, affection or benevolence; a quality which can only exist in strong, deep, and undemonstrative natures. She found that quality in Cassie just from reading her diaries. She also found it in her grandmother and in Andy.

Looking back at Sara she said,

"thank you for visiting grandmother so often...it means so much to her, and to me."

As she drove out of the village she thought again of Andy and how she longed to see him and hear his voice. They had spent Christmas at the cottage and she still savoured every minute of the week they spent together. They walked along the silent laneways, and along the cliffs and beaches arm in arm, savouring every precious moment oblivious to the outside world.

They had time and space to find themselves, to find the inner person, and to savour what was spread before their senses. When daylight faded they would curl up by the turf fire while Mary read drafts of the novel aloud to him. They trod in Cassie O'Connor's footsteps to what remained of the cottage where she had lived and wandered through the derelict rectory; the places of her youth and childhood. They had stood in front of the building that had once been the workhouse, and looked on the solitary cross, the only monument to the resting place of its dead. They had visited the sites of historic interest and saw the broken, scanty remains of Monastic Ireland about them; St Kevin's well, St Kieran's church and the Celtic cross's that was all that remained of the once thriving monasteries. They could visualise the monks illuminating the manuscripts of the Saints, bronze bell, tallow candle and the Latin text recited in the soft tongue of the Gael. Closing their eyes, they could imagine a dawn of a mysterious sun or, a night of a mysterious full moon when all would be restored.

The only trip away from the Donegal cottage came when, at Andy's suggestion they flew to London to see 'Riverdance.' As she watched the wonderful spectacle, Mary remembered now, how proud she had felt of her Irish heritage, the culture and creativity found in music, dance and literature and the amazing contribution of the descendants of the famine who had been cruelly scattered to the four corners of the earth.

It made her even more proud not only of Cassie O'Connor's struggles, but, also of the courage and fortitude of those who had been part of her life and times. Following that visit to London she had once again became totally immersed in the lives of the people from that other time.

She knew that she wouldn't see Andy again until her task was complete, but right now her heart ached with longing for him. They had decided to postpone their decision about their future until she'd finished her writing. But, she already knew what her answer would be. As she turned in past the crumbling gate lodge her thoughts went into a spin, 'what if he has changed his mind about me? I haven't heard from him for two weeks.'

The car moved slowly along the overgrown driveway, coming to a halt at the front of the derelict crumbling mansion. A sycamore tree protruded through the roof space, and grass swayed eerily from the high window ledges. In Mary's head there was that image of a century and a half ago. She could see its grandeur again in her mind's eye, see the fine carriages, the rustling silks of the ladies; the maids lining the steps. Getting out of the car, she stood gazing at its desolate, decayed grandeur while the cows grazed beneath the crumbling edifice.

She walked away from the overgrown driveway, skirting the lake and on towards the dark trees. Recalling the description of the place from Cassie's diary she wondered if the tree where she and Harry carved their initials could still be standing. She scrutinised the barks carefully, but found nothing. 'How could I expect to when almost a century and a half has passed?' she asked herself.

Sitting herself down underneath the most likely looking tree, she let her thoughts drift. There were so many gaps in Cassie's written record of her life and time from the time she and Harry met as two young adults under the tree. Possibly because she had little time to spare as a busy wife and mother. Her love for Harry and later for her children had never dimmed during her long life. They had lived in Saint John for twelve years, returning to Ireland with their three children when Harry's father became ill and was unable to look after his wife any longer. With Marcia already living in Liverpool where Johnny had become a partner in a new shipbuilding enterprise the burden of care had fallen on Harry and Cassie.

Looking back at the earliest memories from Cassie's diary, Mary found it a strange irony that she should be the one to look after her in old age, the woman, who had humiliated and despised her in childhood. 'Get them out of here. God knows what awful diseases they carry,' echoed from the pages of Cassie's diary.

For nearly three years Cassie and her family had lived in the rectory---if that miserable existence of Julia Briggs could have been called living; bed-ridden and fallen into second childhood she posed no threat to Cassie any longer.

And in the process of time their burden was lifted, when one summer day, a small decent funeral left the Rectory for the churchyard, all the comment was, "oh, is she dead? What a relief it must be. Wasn't it good of Cassie to look after her so well." Cassie had written, 'yes, she was dead, and had made no sign, either of repentance, grief or gratitude.' Cassie's description of the Reverend's funeral three years later was in marked contrast to that of his late wife. The people from the entire parish and beyond lined the route to the graveyard to pay homage to the man who had worked selflessly for the people. He had been quick sighted, meeting any sorrows, looked it steadily in the face, knowing neither the coward's dread nor the unbeliever's disguise of pain, worked bravely on, and shared what little he had with those who needed it most.

Mary's thoughts went back to her own cosseted, affluent childhood in New York. She had been given almost everything her heart desired by her indulgent parents and the best college education her father's money could buy. This background made it hard for her to imagine what it felt like to know hunger, poverty, fear and the insecurity that her great great grandmother and her fellow countrymen and women had endured or how it must have felt to board a ship bound for the unknown, in a desperate attempt to survive.

Yet, in some strange way, she had been there in her head and in her heart of that she was sure. Cassie O'Connor's life and times had become mingled with her own. 'How could it be?' she asked herself, when she had gadded around the world hanging on to every utterance of the wealthy, spoiled, unhappy small selection of humanity who had acquired fame either, through accident of birth or lucky breaks. 'Could she go back and fit into that other world again?' she asked herself. Now thoughts of Andy were returning, disturbing her peace of mind and she longed just to see him again. Resting her head against the tree she dozed in the warm sun.

Chapter 23

The Reunion

Andy Medcaff collected his hire car at Aldergrove airport as prearranged and headed North. As he drove along the Glen road flanked on both sides by heather clad hills, he wondered what Mary's reaction to his sudden unannounced arrival might be. Then his thought about the women from his past; relationships that hadn't stood the test of time. From the very beginning he knew that Mary was different; she had been part of his every waking thought since they met two years ago. He knew that she needed this space to be alone to write. Although he tried not to show it, he couldn't deny that he had been hurt when she first told him of her plan to write the story of this ancestor of hers. What was it with people of Irish decent and this obsession about ancestry and the past he had wondered? But the time they spent together a few months ago had helped him to understand that almost life and death compulsion that drove her to complete this project. He had to confess to being deeply touched by this story as she read drafts of her manuscript to him by the turf fire in the Donegal cottage. Her luminous green eyes possessed a warmth and a crystal brightness that sang with joy when she talked about her work and her love for this new place that she now thought of as home.

He felt confused and fearful as the miles sped past bringing him closer to an answer to the question that burned deep into his very being. If she rejected him, then he must accept it with good grace, he told himself. But he wasn't sure if he could.

He drove slowly along the rutted laneway and parked the car in the cottage driveway. Jumping out, he rang the door bell and listened to its echoes tingle and fade away into the distance. A look of quick impatience crossed his face and his eyebrows twitched with a kind of whimsical annoyance when she failed to answer his urgent ring. Going around to the back, he tried the door, it too was locked. Glancing through the kitchen window he noted that the dishes from the last meal were still on the table and this gave him hope.

Dashing back to the car he drove up the lane. Sara McLaughlin was bent over weeding a flower bed when she heard the car pull up. Turning around she said,

"It's Andy as I live and breathe. I only seen Mary a wee while ago an' she said nothing about expecting you."

"She doesn't know. It's a surprise. Would you happen to know where I might find her?"

"Aye. She's away up to the old Hall. Said something about a tree.... Carvings on a tree. Said she read about it in the diary. She got that old portrait of the wee girl you know. Aye, some relation agreed to lend it to her. An' as I said to her, that wee girl had the same eyes as herself. You would have thought she won the lotto she was that excited about it."

"Could you direct me to that Hall please?"

"Aye surely. But, why don't you come in for a drop of tea and wait 'till she comes back."

"Thanks for the offer, but I'd rather see if I could find her."
Looking at him with a knowing twinkle in her eye she said,

"Can't wait eh? Young love's a great thing."

Following Sara's direction carefully, Andy drove through the gateway and crawled along the neglected overgrown driveway. As the ruins of the mansion came into view, he too, imagined its past glories and grandeur that Cassie O'Connor had described in her diary. With relief, he saw Mary's car parked directly in front of the stone steps. Getting out of the car he debated with himself whether to wait by the car or try to find her. He could see the lake in the distance taking his memory back to Cassie's diary where, he had read her account of the meeting with Harry under the tree by the lake. He walked towards the clump of trees skirting the lake, treading carefully amongst the cow pats.

Then he saw her leaning against the bark of the oak tree, her eyes closed as if she were asleep. He had a strong compulsion to run towards her, then thought better of it. As he watched her, he felt unsure and vulnerable and, wondered again about the wisdom of appearing unannounced like this. But he was a man who had caught a tiger by the tail and could not let it go. He walked slowly towards her, his footsteps silent on the damp grass. Not quite awake, she looked up and saw him as if a motion picture had appeared behind her eye lids. Her mouth opened and closed, but no sound came. He held out his hands towards her and smiled. She stood up slowly and flew into his arms.

"Andy. Oh, Andy...I thought you'd forgotten me. You didn't call; answer my messages on your voice mail or anything."

"I had to go to Colorado for three weeks. Tried calling you before I left but your line was always busy. Anyhow, thought you needed time to be alone."
He smiled a somewhat curious smile before kissing her gently on the lips.

"You don't know how much I've missed you," she said softly, and as she looked up at him, she thought they were, in a sense, married by their past, by the year and a half they had been lovers. They stood silently swaying gently with their arms around each other, savouring each others nearness.

"I've got two whole weeks to spend with you," his muffled voice came from over her shoulder. Can I give you a hand with the book in any way?" he asked.

"I'd love that. And I know the very task I'd like you to do for me," she said, as they sat down under the tree.

"Anything. Just say the word."

"Grandma's eyesight has almost gone…and well I was hoping that you might read the manuscript onto audio tape for her."
Looking at her again he smiled,

"sure. But would my voice do it justice?"

"You have the nicest sounding voice in the world. You'd do it justice all right.
Then she asked,

"do you believe in fate?"

"Not sure. Why do you ask?"

"Well, I was half dreaming, half awake a while ago. I was thinking about Cassie and Harry an' you and me. It was all muddled up in my head. This is what she described in her diary. Then you appear out

237

of the blue."

"Or not so blue," he said looking up at the darkening sky.

"If there's a thunderstorm…that'll clinch it."

"What do you mean?"

"Well in the diary…when Cassie and Harry met here there was a thunderstorm, and they sheltered in the summerhouse. It's a bit spooky don't you think?"

When she looked up at him he had an amused grin on his face,

"never really believed much in spooks myself."

"Now you're laughing at me," she said, with a hint of annoyance in her voice.

No sooner were the words spoken, when a loud rumble of thunder pealed loudly and the old tree above them seemed to quiver with it's vibration.

Grabbing her by both hands he pulled her to her feet,

"I've changed my mind…this is spooky, strange, fate or whatever. As I see no summer villa we better make for the car." Then pulling her along by the hand, they ran towards their parked cars.

Driving home through the rain with Andy following behind, Mary couldn't help feeling elated by his impromptu, unexpected appearance. Then came a sudden feeling of gloom. She thought of the number of times he had asked her to make a commitment about their future and how each time she had fobbed him off. He had seemed genuinely delighted to see her again, but, he didn't mention the word love. If he had done, she knew now that she would have told him that she wanted to spend the rest of her life with him. 'But, maybe it's too late, he may have grown tired of waiting or, worse still, found someone else.' Then she reminded herself, that he had come all this way, and surely that accounted for something. She thought again about her compulsion to write this book about Cassie's life and about how much she might have sacrificed in the process; Andy, loss of salary and maybe even her career. But, she could not regret her decision, whatever the consequences; she would never regret this time of her life.

The audio tapes sat in a neat pile, twenty-three in all. Mary and Andy stood looking at them in silence for a few seconds before Andy stacked them neatly into the white cardboard box.

Mary grabbed her coat from the hall stand,

"well here goes. Crunch time."

Andy smiled at her before putting his arm around her shoulder,

"don't look so downcast. This is your big day. You've done it and I'm willing to bet that your grandmother will love every word you've written. It's a wonderful tribute to Cassie O'Connor and to all the other people that were a part of her life and times. In fact it's a tribute to all the Irish people who lived through that time."

"Thank you Andy for having such faith in me. And thank you for doing such a great job at reading it all onto the tapes. No wonder you're hoarse."

With her two hands she gently bent his head forward and kissed him softly on the lips. As he returned her kiss she waited for him to say something; anything that would give her even a hint of his feelings for her. But he said nothing.

"Better head for the nursing home," she said, forcing herself to sound cheerful.

For the next two days Mary and Andy explored their surroundings, walking on the golden, sandy beaches, climbing the heather clad hills, and in the evenings sitting by the turf fires of the local pubs soaking up the atmosphere or listening to the local musicians. No matter how hard she tried, nervous anxiety crept into Mary's consciousness. Anxiety about Andy's changed attitude towards her and about her grandmother's reaction to her book. Then Andy would smile at her in that special way of his that still had the power to turn her legs to jelly. He would squeeze her hand and say, "It'll be OK. She'll love it."

"You've always had the power to read my thoughts," she replied.

"Thought it was only the Celts that possessed that power. Maybe some of that Celtic mysticism has rubbed off on me; at least I can hope," he added, as he drove up to the cottage door.

They had just rid themselves of their coats when the phone rang.

"Is that Mary Jordan?

"Speaking."

"Joan Murphy here from Meadowdunn nursing home, your grandmother would like to see you right away. Oh, and Andy too."

"Tell her we'll be there in an hour or so."

Turning to Andy she said, "seems like she's ready to give her verdict."

His eyes rested on her face for a second, then he put a comforting arm around her shoulders and gave her a gentle squeeze,

"ready?" She nodded, giving him a thin smile.

Mary knocked gently on the cream coloured door of her grandmother's room. When she didn't answer her knock she turned the handle and peered inside. The old woman sat slumped in the chair and with a wild flutter of the heart Mary thought for a second that she was dead. Then she saw her chest move slowly up and down,

"Grandma. Grandma," she said, moving closer to the chair. Suddenly she opened her eyes, staring from one face to the other with a vacant expression. "It's me Grandma. Mary...and Andy. Don't you remember asking for us to come?"

"Of course I remember. I'm not doting yet. Pull up a couple of chairs," she said with a wide sweep of her hand.

As she arranged the chairs, Mary noticed the cassette tapes strewn at her feet, making her heart skip a beat. Had she flung them to the floor in despair, she wondered? Then to Mary's astonishment she asked them about the weather and how they had spent the day without making any reference to the reason for them being here.

"Pick them tapes up in case I stamp on them. I'm that clumsy these days." Then she sighed deeply before going on, "old age is a terrible burden...a terrible burden."

'For God's sake tell me and get it over with,' Mary's inner voice screamed.

"I suppose you'll want to know what I think of your book about Grandma?" she asked, with a mischievous glint in her old eyes. She cleared her throat loudly. "I think it's wonderful. Just wonderful. You took me on a journey that I've tried to imagine in my head for most of my life…only you have the gift of making it real. It's a fitting tribute to Grandma and to our people in their time of sorrow." Then grabbing Mary by the hand she pulled her towards her with surprising strength and kissed her on the cheek. Then turning her gaze to Andy she said, "as for you young man. I thank you. You done a grand job in bringing it all to life for me. You have the most melodious of voices. I suppose toady's generation would call it a sexy voice. Anyhow, thank you."

"It was a pleasure… and an honour," he said feeling humbled by her genuine gratitude. "But mine was the easy job. Mary did all the hard work."

Then looking from one to the other she asked with startling suddenness,

"What about you two. Are you a permanent fixture… or what?" Mary could feel the blood rush to her face,

"oh, Grandma…you are so inquisitive. That's …. personal," she stammered in embarrassment.

"To hell with personal. I want to know. And if you must know I think you are right for one another. Come on… you must know by now. After all you've lived together an' been lovers I'm sure. Unheard of in my day mind you. But I'm not so ancient that I don't know these things."

In the silence that followed Mary stared at the

floor, wished that a hole would appear and consume her.

"Mary." Andy's voice seemed to come from a great distance, "your grandmother is right. We are right for one another, and I've wanted to know for ages how you felt about ... us being permanent. But I was half afraid to ask....didn't want to rush you."

They looked at each other for a few seconds in silence. Then she flung her arms around his neck. "I was waiting for you to ask," she said in a muffled voice.

"Didn't want to rush her. I never heard such poppycock. An' the two of you living together an' sleeping together for God knows how long."

She could feel Andy's shoulders shake with laughter as he listened to the old woman's sarcastic remarks. Mary's thoughts fled back to Cassie's diary when she wrote about the joy that sprigs out of wretchedness.